T0196640

So Bad It
Must Be Good

Also by Nicole Helm

Mile High Romances

Need You Now
Mess with Me
Want You More

Gallagher & Ivy Romances

So Wrong It Must Be Right
So Bad It Must Be Good

So Bad It Must Be Good

Nicole Helm

LYRICAL SHINE
Kensington Publishing Corp.
www.kensingtonbooks.com

LYRICAL SHINE BOOKS are published by

Kensington Publishing Corp.
119 West 40th Street
New York, NY 10018

All Kensington titles, imprints, and distributed lines are available at special quantity discounts for bulk purchases for sales promotion, premiums, fund-raising, educational, or institutional use.

Special book excerpts or customized printings can also be created to fit specific needs. For details, write or phone the office of the Kensington Sales Manager: Kensington Publishing Corp., 119 West 40th Street, New York, NY 10018. Attn. Sales Department. Phone: 1-800-221-2647.

First Electronic Edition: August 2017
eISBN-13: 978-1-5161-0025-5
eISBN-10: 1-5161-0025-5

First Print Edition: August 2017
ISBN-13: 978-1-5161-0026-2
ISBN-10: 1-5161-0026-3

Printed in the United States of America

To all the romance novels that showed a shy girl how to be brave.

Chapter One

Kayla Gallagher stood at the entrance to the brand-new Gallagher & Ivy Farmers' Market with a sharp pang in her chest.

Her baby. Her brainchild. Exactly as she'd planned before her father had gotten his hands on the idea and warped it into something else, but somehow, even after Gallagher's hadn't acquired the land her father had said they needed for this, it existed in Gallagher's small back parking lot.

Every Wednesday afternoon. April through October. A selection of local vendors, all food and crafts grown or made within sixty miles of where they now stood. Opening day, a bustling crowd in the cool April afternoon.

And she had nothing to do with it.

For good reason. You are making a stand.

Except she'd been making a stand for six months now, leaving her position as sustainability manager at Gallagher's Tap Room—her family's pride and joy—and keeping her somewhat toxic family at a distance, and all she felt was empty, lost, and alone.

"Holy shit, Kayla Gallagher, is that you?"

Kayla startled at the deep male voice, trying to place it, trying to hide so no one could see her getting teary over what was no longer hers.

"I'd recognize that red hair anywhere," the man continued, clearly not noticing or caring that she'd tried to escape.

So she had to turn, she had to smile, she had to pretend. *Isn't that the Gallagher way?*

Her heart did an odd flip and drop as a handsome man grinned at her. As though he knew her, but she couldn't . . . Wait. Something about the tiny almost unnoticeable scar at the corner of his mouth, the flashing brown eyes, the familiarity of the *mischief* in them.

"Aiden Patrick?"

The grin widened, flashing those perfect white teeth. Funny how the jitters from being a young teenager could reappear when she was twenty-seven years old.

"You look exactly the same, Carrot," he said, giving her hair a friendly tug, as if they'd seen each other yesterday instead of something like ten years. Maybe more.

Aiden's father had been the handyman to her family's restaurant for as long as she could remember, and when Mr. Patrick's boys had been old enough, he'd started to bring them with him to assist him.

Because Kayla had spent much of her childhood haunting the corners of Gallagher's Tap Room, she'd always been around when they had. She'd had a crush on Aiden for almost the entirety of her teen years, but Aiden had stopped coming with his father something like a decade ago while his brother Liam had stayed on.

"I . . . Well, this is a surprise," Kayla managed, trying to calm her jangling nerves, trying to remind herself she wasn't a little girl mooning after a hot guy anymore.

"Come on, Liam's around here somewhere. You've got to say hi."

"Oh. No, I—" She couldn't go into the farmers' market; she couldn't be seen. Not by anyone with the last name Gallagher if she could help it.

But just like when they were teens and Aiden was supposed to be helping his dad fix something at Gallagher's, Aiden didn't pay any mind. Aiden marched to the beat of his own drum, and Kayla had always been so infatuated by him if for that alone.

The grin, the fact he'd looked at her and her infinitely more confident cousin, Dinah, with at least the same amount of teenage flirtation, had always had her trailing after him like a puppy.

She was trying to change her life—herself—but she was becoming increasingly aware that some things didn't change.

"Our boy's got himself a little side business when he's not helping Dad out with the old ball and chain. Though you're a part of your old ball and chain, aren't you? You've probably seen each other."

"Oh, well—"

"Here we are! Liam! Look who I found."

Kayla would have stayed hidden behind Aiden, but he didn't let her, giving her a nudge toward a booth inside the market. The table was filled with little wooden figures and knickknacks, and Kayla found herself smiling against her will at a tiny grinning bear.

"Hello, Ms. Gallagher."

She could remember every moment she'd spent in the company of Liam Patrick because he always used that cool, professional tone with her. He always looked at her somewhat blankly with shocking blue eyes, and she always got so tongue-tied around him she couldn't speak.

Her body reacted to Liam, unfavorably. She felt all short of breath and nervous and *ungainly.* While she'd never been a particularly smooth or confident person, only Liam had ever made her feel *wrong*.

Her family could make her feel small, invisible, unimportant. Her friends could make her feel like a lonely robot who wasn't allowed to have problems of her own. Aiden could make her feel like a fluttering, giggling schoolgirl.

But only Liam Patrick had ever made her feel like she was in the wrong spot, at the wrong time and it was her own fault.

She did not care for him at *all*. But she smiled. "Hi, Liam. I didn't realize you were . . ." Artistic, for starters. Buying booth space at Gallagher's newest venture either.

"It's a hobby," he said flatly, those ice-blue eyes such a contrast to the thick black hair on his head and the scruff on his face. He should have been handsome, but he was so *severe*.

Aiden smiled, and Aiden flirted, and Liam always stared at her as if she were someone to avoid like the plague.

And *insisted* on calling her Ms. Gallagher when he couldn't.

"You know, I'd prefer it if you call me Kayla," she said, surprising both men, and herself for that matter. But she was taking a stand, and if six months in she still felt lost and alone, well, she needed to do something about it, not expect the world to change to suit her.

Liam said nothing to that. Aiden grinned. Yes, some things did not change with time, but she would. She was *trying*.

"I've got to get going. I've got an appointment, but give me your phone number, Carrot. We've got years to catch up on." Aiden pulled his phone out of his pocket.

This all felt so surreal. Being in the market she'd designed, but now had no part of, running into her teenage crush, Liam's usual unnerving and steady stare, but Kayla rattled off her phone number and plastered a smile on her face.

"I'll call you," Aiden said, leaning in and brushing an overly familiar kiss across her cheek.

Kayla could only stare after him as he strode away, heat infusing her cheeks, an odd discomfort settling in her chest.

She wasn't sure how long she stared after him before Liam cleared his throat. She was sure she was already blushing. God knew what terrible shade of red she'd turn now. She swallowed and turned to face Liam.

His expression was still blank and unreadable, and in a way that was nice. If he was being judgmental or making fun of her, he was doing it all on the inside.

She glanced down at the table again, all manner of beautiful things carved into wood. Figurines, spoons, and bowls, even rolling pins. It was a veritable treasure trove, but she kept looking back at the smiling bear.

She closed her hand over it, because it was better than looking at Liam and all his stern blankness. "I'd like to buy it," she said with a little nod, lifting her gaze to his.

His dark eyebrows drew together, forming a deep line across his forehead. "Why?"

She blinked. "It's cute. It made me smile."

"It's a child's toy."

This time she outright frowned at him, and though her instinct was to smooth it away and smile politely, she pushed that instinct down and kept up the frown. "Do you do this to all your customers? I don't think you'll have much success."

His scowl tightened, and she'd never understand why *this* happened between them. Tension and discomfort and a weird prickling across her skin that she'd never felt with anyone else.

It wasn't that she didn't like him; though maybe he didn't like her. She didn't know why he'd have reason not to, but maybe some people didn't need reasons.

"Ten dollars," he finally said gruffly.

Eesh. It wasn't much, but she was on a tight budget. She'd only been taking little temporary jobs since she'd left Gallagher's, living mostly off her savings, and it was dwindling . . . hard.

But for some reason she could not back down to Liam Patrick and his *It's a child's toy* jerk face. So she scrounged around in her purse for ten bucks.

Ten. For a child's toy.

"I also accept Visa."

Again, Kayla's first instinct was to smooth her own irritation away before it showed, and it was so frustrating that she couldn't wipe that part of herself out. That she always tried to act like she was *fine* when she was so far from it.

She swallowed at the tightness in her throat, because maybe she was just never going to be fine.

"Look, you don't have to—"

Mortified that he'd clearly not only realized she was upset, but misconstrued the reason, Kayla thrust her credit card at him.

"I—"

"I want a receipt," she countered, not allowing him to take back the price or the sale. She thrust the card at him again and he took it with a sigh.

He grumbled something, but she didn't catch it, and honestly that was probably for the best. He ran the card through the attachment on his phone before handing it back to her.

"I can wrap it for you," he said, nodding toward the figurine she'd grabbed.

She closed her fingers tighter around the bear. "No, this will be fine." Maybe it could be something of a talisman. Because if things didn't change soon . . .

She glanced back at the brick building of Gallagher's Tap Room that loomed behind her. She couldn't go back.

So she had to move forward.

"Goodbye, Liam."

"I thought you wanted a receipt."

She shook her head, stepping away from his table, away from Gallagher's. "No, I'm fine." She would be. She *would* be.

Liam stepped into his parents' house after dropping off his stock at home. He hadn't told either of them about his foray into selling his hobby, and he didn't plan to. The last thing he needed was Dad thinking his focus was split from their handyman business.

Liam was used to keeping things from his parents, from the people he loved. He'd learned to keep hopes and dreams and things of that nature to himself, and do what needed to be done. That was his role in the Patrick clan, and he took it very seriously.

They all took their roles seriously, he supposed. Mom protested things, Dad fixed things, and neither of them would ever submit to "suburban boredom." Liam sometimes wished they would, but he never told them that.

Aiden was the "free spirit" and the one who got to do whatever the hell he damn well pleased, and Liam was the good son. The dutiful son. The partner. He'd stood up and been everything his older brother hadn't been.

He heard laughing from the kitchen, Aiden and Mom, because somehow Aiden was still the hero. Liam knew he was appreciated, but he was never . . . that other thing. He'd never been able to figure out what it was, what they gave Aiden that they didn't give him. He only knew it existed.

Liam didn't care for the reminder he could be as childish as his brother, but a bitterness lingered any time Aiden was around.

"Liam? Is that you? We're in the kitchen," Mom called.

He might have some childhood bitterness toward his brother, but that didn't mean he had to show it. Just another thing to keep to himself. Just another thing to swallow down and act like it didn't matter.

Because it didn't *matter*, not in a way he could change, so there was no use dwelling.

Liam pushed out a breath, trying to force out old, useless feelings. He focused on the fact that he loved his family wholeheartedly, with everything he was. With everything he had. He made sacrifices not because he had to, but because it was a choice he made to make the people in his family happy.

He'd always felt that way, and Dad's heart attack two years ago had only cemented that certainty. He'd made promises in that hospital room, to his father, to God, to himself.

So maybe parts of him were bitter, but he wouldn't change a damn thing. His family's happiness was the most important thing.

And when will you worry about your own happiness?

He didn't want to contemplate that. So he stepped in the kitchen with his best approximation of a smile.

"There you are, slowpoke. Your father is still with the Mosleys, and you know they'll feed him dinner. I was going to make you boys something, but I actually have to go. My group is meeting at Monsanto."

"Should we be prepared to have to bail you out?"

Mom patted Aiden's cheek, smiling. "You never know! Plenty of food in the fridge. We'll plan family dinner another night." She hurried out of the kitchen without a second glance, clearly in crusader mode.

"I don't know if we should be encouraging her," Liam said, feeling exhausted because God knew Mom getting arrested wasn't that far out of the realm of possibility.

"Like she needs encouraging," Aiden replied, opening the fridge and poking around. "Let's go out to eat. I'm starving and this all looks far too healthy."

"You're just going to live here then?" Liam asked, and immediately regretted it, because it was none of his business. Aiden living at home was none of his damn business.

"Hello, judgmental brother," Aiden returned, closing the fridge, but he grinned like he didn't give a shit.

Because Aiden straight out didn't. Not about much beyond himself. Which wasn't fair, in the least, but it was true, and Liam wasn't very good at ignoring the truth.

"I'm not judg—"

"I'm only here until I figure out what my next move is. Although right now my next move is Kayla Gallagher. Hey, why are you always such a dick to her?"

"I'm a dick to everyone," Liam grumbled. Which was an exaggeration, but he didn't want to think about Kayla Gallagher.

"Sure, but she's . . ." Aiden shook his head and Liam hated that his gut could still twist just like it had when he'd been a kid.

Kayla Gallagher was *something*. Very nearly ethereal. Sweet and shy, and she'd never failed to make him feel like a plodding, cardboard asshole. Especially, *especially* when Aiden was around.

Liam felt superior to his brother in just about every way. Aiden ran away and came back home with a regularity Liam had given up trying to change. Liam, on the other hand, always stayed put. He had partnered with his father in the family business because it was the right thing to do. He'd been at Dad's bedside after the heart attack, and he'd kept Patrick's Patch-ups going through Dad's recovery. He did the *right* thing, instead of whatever the hell he wanted to do.

But Kayla Gallagher had been the one chink in his superiority for as long as he could remember, and the worst part was he didn't have a fucking clue as to why.

He did not have trouble with women. He could be charming. He could smile.

Except around *her*.

"Well, don't be so hard on her. Once I get out of my current situation, I will be barking up that tree, and I don't need her hating my brother in my way."

"What does any of that mean?" Liam asked, feeling a headache pound at his temples.

"It means Kayla Gallagher is mine. So don't ruin things for me. Simple."

"What situation do you need to take care of before she's . . . yours." He made air quotes with his fingers as he said *yours,* trying to get a bit of a rise out of Aiden, but Aiden never stopped smiling.

"Let's just say I may be involved with someone else right now, but I'll get that sorted out. Kayla has always been that something special, and now I'll finally be around to do something about it."

"I'm sure she's been chastely waiting for you," Liam replied deadpan.

"Don't be jealous women like me better, Liam. It doesn't suit you."

"Women like me just fine." Which was true. But hell if he didn't feel fifteen and gawky again just at the very appearance of Kayla Gallagher.

Of course, signing up for the Gallagher & Ivy Farmers' Market, he'd known he might run into her again. Any time he got called in to do a repair at Gallagher's, he kept his eyes open for the possibility of catching a glimpse of her red hair.

But that was before Aiden had come home after being gone the past year, because per usual, Aiden existed at the center of all Liam's problems, fair or not. He likely always would.

Someday . . . Liam was tired of his own somedays. Someday didn't matter. What mattered was today, and today he was living up to every promise he'd ever made. It was his satisfaction at the end of the day, and even his brother couldn't change that.

"So let's go eat? Gallagher's?"

"I'm not going to Gallagher's to eat." Not with Aiden. "Like you said, if you want Kayla, you don't want me anywhere near her."

It might not be for reasons that made any sense to him, but he did not know how to be around that woman. So he found the best answer was to just not be.

Chapter Two

Kayla looked at herself in the mirror. Her nerves were out of control, but dates always made her nervous. She hadn't been on one in a while either. She'd been focusing on herself. Focusing on changing her life. She didn't think adding a man before she did that was very smart, but . . . Well, when the man was Aiden Patrick, she wasn't sure she had much of a choice.

Who could say no to a childhood fantasy come to life? She hadn't seen him in something like ten years and still he *looked* like a fantasy come to life, even without the teenage crush factoring in.

Tall, broad, a sort of effortless charm that oozed out of his smile. He was always at ease, and Kayla couldn't help but admire the way Aiden did whatever he wanted to do regardless of anyone else.

Then there were the blue eyes . . .

Brown eyes. *Brown.*

She blew out a breath hard enough that it ruffled the hair falling around her cheeks.

Why she kept thinking about Liam's blue eyes when she was *trying* to think about Aiden was admittedly slightly concerning. Except Liam was the last Patrick she'd seen. It was like a dream where you didn't control what you saw. It was a mix of your subconscious and the things you'd thought of that day.

But Aiden had called her this afternoon and asked if she was free for drinks tonight, and she was and . . .

She smoothed down her dress again, feeling a little sick.

Quite honestly the conversation with Aiden had been weird. He did a lot of talking about his travels, the things he'd seen and the places he'd been, and she knew that was supposed to be interesting.

But she felt like she was attending a play, a performance. It hadn't been particularly genuine.

Which was probably just because she was nervous. She was nervous talking to Aiden on the phone. She was nervous about talking to him tonight. So that was why it felt weird. It was *her*.

Everything was fine and she was going on a date with Aiden Patrick. Meeting him at some swanky bar and they were going to have drinks and a great time.

Still, she couldn't bring herself to smile. In a moment like this, she missed talking to Dinah. Talking with her cousin and best friend had always been her predate ritual, one that had calmed her enough to have a few decent relationships in her twenties.

Dinah would have good advice. She'd know just what to wear and what to say.

But Kayla had come to something of an epiphany last year. She had relied far too much on her cousin and had let Dinah lead her around by the nose as a result. It wasn't Dinah's fault in the least, but in order to protect herself and try for this new life, Kayla'd had to break the tie and take a step back.

It had been admittedly easier due to the fact Dinah was so disgustingly in love. Due to the fact Dinah had disobeyed Grandmother, and somehow still had a job with Gallagher's.

But no matter how many times Kayla told herself jealousy was a waste of an emotion, and she didn't want Dinah's life anyway, it ached a little bit. The loss, the things Dinah had. Which was why cutting all things Gallagher out of her life had been necessary. She needed to figure out who *she* was.

So why haven't you yet?

"You are not thinking about this," she told herself firmly in the mirror. "You are not depressing yourself. Not tonight. Tonight is a fresh start."

She turned away from the mirror and looked at the little bear figurine she'd placed on her dresser. It was hard to believe Liam had made that with his own two hands. She wasn't sure she'd ever seen him smile, except that polite smile when handing Grandmother the bill.

He was a serious guy, but he'd made this grinning bear. This child's toy.

Why the hell was she thinking about Liam again? All Liam had ever done was make her feel crazy awkward and uncomfortable for a lot of years.

She was going on a date with *Aiden Patrick,* and that was her focus. She just had to get in her car, drive to the bar, and everything would be great. Fresh start. Dates and cute guys and finding herself. Maybe the past six months had been about healing and separating, and now she had to start building.

Yes, that was it. She had done her deconstruction project, and now she was going to reconstruct. To build the life she wanted. Not a Gallagher life, but a Kayla life.

Maybe if things went well with Aiden, she'd be able to figure out what she needed. Maybe getting out there and meeting new people was the actual answer, instead of spending six months working and navel gazing.

She smiled, emboldened, and grabbed her purse and keys.

It would be a good night. Come hell or high water.

"You want me to do *what*?" Liam very nearly pulled the phone away from his ear to make sure it was actually his brother on the line and not, say, an alien.

"I'm caught up, and I don't want to stand her up."

Liam shook his head, trying to work through his brother's nonsense. This was what he got for bringing his cell into his workshop. Which was a dilapidated detached garage, all in all, but he'd made it into a functional space to do his woodworking. "Call her and tell her you can't make it."

"You can't leave a hot woman in a bar by herself stood up. My God, half the dumbasses in the joint would have a shot with her."

"So, to be clear, you want me to go on your date in your stead," Liam returned, his voice as flat and dispassionate as he could possibly manage.

He wished he could *feel* all that on the inside, because on the inside he felt pretty fucked up. Chest tight. Jittering heartbeat. Knots tying in his gut.

"Hell no. You go. You explain the situation. You make sure she leaves, and then you're free to hit on any other woman who's been stood up."

"I'm supposed to leave my work—"

"Thought it was a hobby," Aiden interrupted, the smugness nearly oozing across the connection.

"All so I can make sure some other guy doesn't hit on the woman you somehow have it in your head is yours. But are standing up for mysterious reasons."

"Liam," Aiden said, his voice dropping into a rare serious tone, "I don't ask you for much."

Which was true. Aiden asked him for things approximately never. He didn't ask, but he made it impossible for Liam to walk away from that need to fix, to help. Even knowing Aiden was a master manipulator.

"Fine," he grumbled. Because he was a weak moron.

Because you want to see her without him around.

He pushed both thoughts away. Firmly. "If it takes more than fifteen minutes, I am leaving her to the wolves. Got it?"

"Sure you are, brother," Aiden returned jovially. "I'll expect a full report tomorrow."

"Tomorrow? Where the hell are you?"

But there was no response, just the beep of his phone telling him the other caller had ended the conversation.

Liam irritably tossed his phone on the worktable. He scowled at what he'd been working on. Because he'd *meant* to make a pair of serving spoons since he'd sold out on Wednesday, but . . .

He'd ended up starting another bear figurine. To *replace* the one Kayla had bought, not to match it.

Now he had to go to some bar in fucking Central West End and somehow explain to a woman he couldn't seem to say three charming words strung together to that his brother would not be showing up.

"You could try saying no once in a while, you helpless fuck," he muttered to himself as he put away his woodworking equipment.

But it wasn't in his nature. Turning down a plea for help, and maybe . . . maybe actually doing something for his older brother would help Liam get over all those old fractures of bitterness. If he could say he had a hand in helping Aiden have a chance with Kayla, well, maybe it would give him the same satisfaction he got out of being the "Son" in Patrick & Son Patch-ups.

Too bad the idea of Aiden and Kayla left a sick feeling in his stomach as he changed into clean jeans and a shirt that didn't look like he'd owned it for ten years. Which was a challenge to find considering his life was fixing things and carving things.

He drove from his house in South City to the bustling Central West End, irritated by just about everything, because irritation covered up that other thing in his chest and gut. And since he wasn't a pansy-ass, he'd take irritation over the rest any damn day.

He swore under his breath while trying to find parking, then swore some more as he walked through the brisk April evening looking for the whiskey bar his brother had picked out.

Once he arrived, it didn't take but a cursory glimpse around to find Kayla's shining beacon of red hair. It was darker than when they'd been teenagers, no longer the flaming orange that had earned her Aiden's Carrot nickname.

Did she like that? He'd only ever hated any of Aiden's nicknames for him. Of course they were names like Reverend Tight Ass and President Boring, but Carrot wasn't exactly flattering.

Neither was the look on Kayla's face as he approached. *Great.*

Kayla fidgeted on the bar stool, smoothing her hands down over the dress that covered her thighs. She looked so damn elegant, and that was the sheer opposite of everything he was or could ever hope to be.

Damn Aiden to hell and back for making him do this.

"Hi, Kayla."

"Um, hi," she greeted him, craning her head around, clearly looking for any sign of Aiden. Or maybe just an escape route. "I was expecting—"

"Aiden called me earlier. He got caught up and couldn't get away, and he asked me to come tell you that."

Kayla's pale red eyebrows drew together. "He couldn't have called me?"

"I guess he thought it would be better if the message was delivered in person."

She outright frowned at that. "He'd be wrong," she muttered.

Liam shouldn't be shocked by her reaction. Hell, he'd had that reaction when Aiden had asked him to do this. Still, something about it twisted one of those knots in his gut tighter.

"I know that it doesn't make much sense, but Aiden asked me for a favor, and I couldn't . . ."

She studied him with that same furrowed brow, and it felt uncomfortably like she could see through him a little too easily. He shifted on his feet.

"You couldn't say no," she supplied for him. "You know, I made it my mission about six months ago to say no, as much as I possibly could."

"How's that going for you?"

She huffed out a breath, almost a laugh but not jovial enough to constitute one. "Not great. Maybe I should've made yes my mission. Or . . ." She shook her head, shimmering red waves of hair brushing across her shoulder blades.

Damn mesmerizing.

"You don't want to hear me yammer on about my problems," she said with a dismissive wave of her hand. "Thanks for being the messenger, really. I don't want to keep you."

Liam could see two choices very clearly ahead of him. On the one hand, he could say no he didn't. He could tell her he'd walk her to her car, and that would be the extent of that.

But she looked so sad, so vulnerable, and hell if he'd ever been able to walk away from offering someone help. "I don't mind," he said, awkwardly sliding into the bar stool next to her. "I'll buy you a drink."

At her shocked expression, he looked away. He was not this stiff, awkward guy, and he wasn't going to let her keep making him into that. He was offering an ear, a shoulder. Something he'd offered to his parents, his friends—hell, half the clients of Patrick & Son unloaded their problems on him, if only for a sounding board.

But Kayla just kept staring at him, and he couldn't stop himself from another awkward fidget. He cleared his throat. "If you want, that is."

She took a deep breath, her gaze going to the shelves of liquor bottles behind the bar, before it returned to him.

"You know what I really want?" she asked, leaning toward him and looking intent and serious. Her blue eyes were darker than his, so dark it almost looked like there was black in them, but her lashes were some fairy dust gold.

And he'd officially lost his mind. He cleared his throat. "Uh, what?"

"I want to get drunk in a bar. I have never done that before. The only time I've been drunk is sharing a bottle of wine with Dinah on my couch, or hers."

Drunk. Kayla wanted to get drunk. In a bar.

With him? He doubted it.

"If you want to call Dinah instead, I won't be offended. Obviously, you probably shouldn't get drunk alone with no way to get home."

She cocked her head, and he'd seen that look from his brother.

"And maybe I should mind my own business because I'm not your keeper," he said, before she could.

Her pretty mouth, painted a deep shade of mesmerizing red, curved into a smile. "I wouldn't mind a keeper." Her cheeks flushed pink. "I mean, that is, I'd like company and I can't call Dinah and . . ." Everything about her dimmed, smile gone, blush gone. She looked pale and sad and lonely.

It wasn't hard to recognize those emotions on someone else. Not hard at all.

"So, I'll, uh, buy you a drink then."

She took a deep breath and looked back behind the bar. "Okay." She gave a nervous little nod. "Okay. We could do that." She brushed some hair behind her shoulder and chewed on her bottom lip before sliding a glance at him. "You don't have anywhere to be?"

He shrugged. "I was just working." At her blink of surprise he realized he had to explain *which* work he'd been doing, not that he'd left a fix-it job to do his brother's bidding. "Wood carving. It's actually . . . a hobby, not . . ."

"You're very good," she supplied when he trailed off.

He ignored the frisson of pleasure the compliment gave him because what did it matter? It *was* a hobby. "Thanks. So, drink?" He motioned to the bartender and ordered a beer, and Kayla ordered some fruity girl drink.

And Liam was officially out of conversation. Christ. What did he talk to any other women about? It deserted him, like she had some kind of voodoo that leaked any ease he had with people right out when she was around.

"Can I . . . Can I ask you an awkward question?" she said, not looking at him, but instead smiling politely at the bartender as he slid her glass toward her.

"Only if I can give an awkward answer," Liam replied, bringing the bottle of beer he'd been given to his lips.

She laughed, as if she was surprised he could say something moderately humorous. "So, um, you know, I've seen you with other people. Like my grandmother. I've *watched* you charm the pants off her, but with me you're . . . Well, did I do something somewhere along the line? Offend you in some way?"

He almost choked on the sip of beer he'd taken. "What? No. Why would you think that?"

She looked hard at her drink. "I don't know. It's just . . . It seems to be *me*. You were always nice to Dinah, easy. And I once watched you charm my grandmother. My *grandmother*. *I* can't charm my grandmother, but she smiled at you."

"It's actually quite easy to charm your grandmother when you accept she's going to hate you no matter what you say."

Kayla laughed, the hint of surprise in it making him wonder what it sounded like if she just laughed without being shocked he was the one making her do it.

"Anyway. Everyone knows Aiden got all the charm."

"What did that leave you with?"

He smiled wryly. "Everything else."

Again, she laughed, and it was something like a drug. He wanted to keep feeling that little jolt when the bright sound tumbled out of her. He wanted her to keep smiling at him like . . .

Well, like he wasn't the dimmer star in Aiden's far more interesting universe.

"You haven't been around lately. Gallagher's, that is." He'd heard, because people didn't always hold their tongues around someone fixing their sink or floorboard, that Kayla had left her position with Gallagher's, but even the loosest of lips hadn't known why.

Her smile faded, the pretty tint of pink in her cheeks going pale again. Because he'd stepped in it, hadn't he? Seriously, what was his deal?

"No, I haven't. And I won't be."

"There a story behind that?" he asked, not because he was nosy, but because some people needed to be asked to unload their problems.

She slid him a glance. "What do you think of the Gallaghers? I mean, not the brewery or the restaurant, but *us*?"

Liam rubbed a hand over his beard, because being put on the spot was never fun. Even when Kayla was the one doing it. "Well . . ."

"Tell the truth. Just whatever you think. It won't hurt my feelings, I promise."

Yeah, right. People didn't want honesty half as much as they thought they did. "There are some complex family dynamics there. But, you know, any time you mix family with business, that's going to happen. I love working with my dad, but it's complicated."

"What if you didn't love it?"

"Huh?"

She polished off her drink and motioned for the bartender to give her another. Apparently she was serious about this getting-drunk thing, which meant he had to be serious about making sure she got home okay.

Whether he told her that or not, she'd officially become his responsibility. If that was a little warped, he'd deal with it later. Maybe he'd seek therapy in his retirement. Or on his deathbed.

"If you didn't love it, if you actually thought working with your family was slowly killing you from the inside out, would you stay?"

It hit a weird spot in his chest, one he had no interest in examining, so he took a deep drink of his beer and tried to formulate some kind of lie.

Chapter Three

When Liam didn't answer her question, Kayla forced herself to look at him. Truth be told, meeting that ice-blue gaze was hard. It made her want to fidget outwardly as much as her organs seemed to fidget inside her body.

But she was *fascinated* by his reaction to her question. No answer, he'd gone almost unnaturally still in the crowded, noisy bar.

Eventually he cleared his throat and frowned down at his hands, which were linked around his beer bottle.

He had rough hands, all beat up, nicked. She imagined doing the intricate woodwork of his hobby would result in a lot of that, and maybe handyman work would too. But there was something oddly compelling about that roughness, about the visible representation of all the work he did.

Don't be weird, Kayla.

"I guess I don't quite understand what you're asking me," he finally said, completely unconvincingly. He wouldn't have had such an outward reaction to the question if he didn't understand it.

Wasn't that interesting? She'd never spent much time considering what kind of person Liam might be. She was usually too busy feeling weird around him.

"So working with your dad is wonderful and perfect?"

"Of course not. Nothing's perfect. I could do my woodworking full time and it still wouldn't be perfect."

"So the woodworking is what you'd rather be doing?"

"No! No, that's not what I meant."

"Defensive much?"

He cocked his head, that blue gaze meeting hers, something like surprise and, maybe it was silly to read into a look, but *interest.*

You're being really weird now.

But he just kept *staring*. "What?" she asked, because maybe he would tell her what this was. This thing rattling around in her chest that she didn't understand at all. She'd always assumed it was discomfort, a special kind only Liam Patrick brought out.

It was different though. It had always been different.

"I just . . ." He shook his head. "You're different than you used to be."

Her mouth curved, because he couldn't have said a thing that would have pleased her more. Different. God, she was trying. "You really think so?"

"Yeah, you're . . . It's the thing. That you were asking about. The 'me treating you differently' thing. Your grandmother, your father, even Dinah, they were . . . I mean, Dinah's nice enough and all, but they were all so purposeful. Strong. They seem untouchable. And you . . ."

Kayla's smile died. Yes, she was none of those things. The odd man out of that Gallagher *toughness*. Grandmother had always said so.

"You always seemed rather fragile, I guess, and I can fix a problem, a stove, a window. I can fix just about anything that's broken, but I've never known how to *keep* something from breaking. So I was never quite comfortable around you."

Kayla felt cracked open a little. She'd never considered herself *fragile*, but hadn't she been? Hadn't she always been cowering in the shadows trying not to break?

"See? I offended you. But that's on me. It was never something you did. It's just me."

"Or my fragility."

He closed his eyes. "You're proving my point that I was right to have kept my mouth shut all those years."

She downed the next drink, concentrating on the warmth blooming in her chest, the way her limbs were starting to feel a tad heavy. Maybe she could drink her way into a new life, a new personality, or a new future.

Anything was better than this constant feeling of failure. *Fragile*. Everyone thought she was fragile or unimportant or . . .

"Hey."

If it had just been his voice, an obnoxiously gentle note to it, she probably wouldn't have stopped her inner wallowing. But he *touched* her. It was featherlight, almost as if he were afraid to do it, just the very tip of his pinky finger resting on the knuckle of hers.

Something like a shudder moved through her, and she couldn't explain why or even what it was. But something about his finger on hers, no matter how barely it rested there, was like a thunderclap. A *moment* that resounded within her, reverberating and booming.

She must be drunk already.

"You shouldn't take anything *I* say to heart. I'm an idiot."

She glanced over at him. He seemed so *genuinely* concerned that something he'd said had made her sad. Troubled that he might have said something that hurt her feelings.

No one cared if they hurt her feelings. Not in the Gallagher clan, where everything was about what could further the business. Not with her friends, who would call her the poor little rich girl if she mentioned her dissatisfaction with things.

Even Dinah, though she could be counted on to be a solid rock if Kayla asked, didn't go out of her way to *see* when she'd hurt Kayla. Not like this.

She looked down at his finger on hers again. He had a bright white scar across his knuckle and a scrape along the side of his hand.

He pulled his hand away, but she impulsively grabbed it. It was probably weird, but there was enough of a buzz in her brain that the knowledge that it was weird got drowned out and she curled her pale, unmarked fingers around his tan, scuffed ones.

"Would you teach me?" she asked, squeezing his hand, looking at him with the most imploring look she could muster.

"Uh, teach you what?" he asked, not so subtly trying to pull his hand away.

She held on tighter. She needed that connection. She needed *help*, and though it seemed strange and out there, she decided Liam Patrick was just the man to do it.

"How to make the figurines. Like the bear."

"You want me to teach you woodworking?"

"Yes." She thrust the hand that wasn't holding his into his face. "Look at my hands. What do you see?"

"Um. Well. I see my eye getting poked in about five seconds." He wrapped his free hand around her waving hand and pressed it to the bar.

"These hands have done *nothing*. Nothing! I've never built anything or shaped anything. All they've ever done is typed and made phone calls and planted a freaking basil plant in a tiny pot on my windowsill. They need to *do*."

"There are lots of things you could do without . . . well, me."

"But you're perfect. Look at *your* hands. They're beat up. You've *done* things with them. You . . . you make the most beautiful things. I want to make something. It doesn't have to be beautiful. It just has to be something." The idea was snowballing through her chest like she'd found a pot of gold, because it felt like a *treasure,* this idea.

"Kayla."

But she paid him no mind. She just kept talking. Which was funny, and made that giddiness flutter harder and more potent through her. She never just *kept* talking. "I was thinking when I was getting ready that I've spent the past few months wallowing in leaving Gallagher's and how that stage needed to be over and I need to *build* my life."

She thrust her hand into his face again and this time when he grabbed it, he curled his fingers around her wrist. Her pulse jumped, her *heart* jumped, but she was too excited about her idea to wonder about that.

"So you can teach me how to make something with my hands. And Carter can teach me how to grow something. And . . . Yes, I will start *doing*. It's the *answer*."

"Who's Carter?"

"Dinah's boyfriend. He has a little urban farm right by Gallagher's." She waved in the general direction of that world. A world she didn't feel a part of, but the trouble was she didn't feel like part of any world.

Which meant she had to *change*. Not just herself, but what she did. "Let's go."

"Kayla." It was his turn to squeeze her hands. "You've been drinking. I can't teach you much when you're halfway to being drunk." He released her hands. "Maybe more than halfway," he muttered.

"Okay, that's fair." It didn't burst her bubble though because this was a plan. *This* was what she'd been waiting for. "Tomorrow morning then."

Liam laughed, then seemed to realize she was serious. "Honey, two more of those and you won't be in any shape in the morning to do much of anything."

The word *honey* rolled off his tongue so easily, but it settled somewhere in her rib cage, like a fish caught in a net. Wiggling, uncomfortable.

Honey.

She shook that word and the very nearly flirtatious way he'd said it away, taking another gulp of her drink to remind herself of the point. "Tomorrow night, then," she decided resolutely.

"I can't teach you in a night how to carve things out of wood. It takes time to learn the tools, to figure it all out."

"I have nothing but time."

He opened his mouth as if to argue with her, but then he simply closed it.

"Please," she offered, flashing him her most winsome smile.

"You really think this is the answer to whatever is wrong, don't you?"

"No, but I think it's a start." She needed a *start*. A foundation. She needed to do. Maybe in the doing she could change or grow. Maybe she wouldn't, but at least it would be acting in some way.

"All right. I'll . . . see what I can teach you."

She made a squeak and impulsively leaned forward and gave him a quick hug. She realized midsqueeze that hugging was not a normal response. That he smelled like wood and beer and maybe soap.

That something inside her chest shifted, eased, *sighed*.

Clearly the booze was working its way through her. She pulled back abruptly and awkwardly waved to the bartender. "Two menus, please," she called before turning a completely forced smile on Liam. "I'm *starving*. Let's eat."

She noticed Liam looked a little deer-in-the-headlights, but she chose to ignore it. Because he was going to teach her how to work wood. Literal wood. Not figurative . . .

"And one more drink, please," she said to the bartender as he handed them menus. She was definitely going to need more to drink.

Liam was pretty certain one of the circles of hell was gorgeous, off-limits women drunkenly plastering themselves all over a guy.

Because it was *hell* having Kayla Gallagher lean against him, soft and warm, smelling like flowers or sunshine or some shit. He tried to maneuver her around the groups of people without touching too much of her, but she kept stumbling and he'd have to wind his arm around her waist and then she'd *lean*.

Shit, hell, and damn.

"You have to let me . . ." She trailed off as she bumped into some couple and Liam tightened his grasp on her, apologizing to the people through gritted teeth.

Her hair kept brushing against his neck, and her hands kept trailing across his chest and abdomen like . . .

Well, he couldn't afford to think too much about what it was like. He had to get the very drunk woman home, and hope like hell she forgot everything about this night and his promise to teach her some woodworking.

What the hell had he been thinking agreeing to that? Dark blue eyes, sweet smile, and for once feeling like he had something to offer Kayla Gallagher.

Damn.

"Oh, it's nice out here," Kayla said, breathing right against his neck as they step-stumbled out of the crowded bar.

"It's freezing," he muttered, having to tighten his grip around her waist again as they maneuvered down the sidewalk.

She only laughed, the sound of it mixing with all the other Friday night revelers.

"Oh!" Kayla stopped abruptly, causing him to stumble to a stop and endure some not so pleasant words from other people walking down the sidewalk. "I have to pay you."

"Pay me?" He nudged her into walking again, trying to think about anything other than the soft give of her body.

"For the drinks. I spent *a lot* of money on drinks. You weren't even supposed to be my date."

"Yeah, I'm aware."

"See? I have to pay you." She shoved her hands into the pockets of her dress, except she kept *trying* to. She missed with one hand, all but grazed his crotch with the second, and this was just definitely hell on earth.

"No, that's not what . . . I don't need you to pay me," he said firmly, pushing her hand away from an imminent danger zone. He hadn't meant he was aware she'd bought a lot of booze. He'd meant he was *very* aware he was not her date.

His brother was. So any shit going on *in* his danger zone was his own shit to take care of. *After* he got the drunk woman currently torturing him safely home.

"But—"

"You are *not* paying me, so stop trying." He upped their pace, even though it wasn't wise with her as stumbling as she was. But at this point, the quicker he got her to his truck, the quicker he could get his hands off her and her hands would be less of a liability, so to speak.

"Here's my truck," he said, taking his arm from around her waist. He pulled his keys out of his pocket. "Where do you live?"

She blinked at him, swaying slightly on her own two feet. "In an apartment."

"Where?"

She squinted, taking an unsteady step toward the curb, swaying a little too dangerously toward the edge. She was going to sprain a damn ankle.

Liam gritted his teeth and reached out to steady her. One hand on either hip. Hell. Hell. Hell.

She gave a sigh, her gaze slowly—*really slowly*, like she was paying very close attention—moved from his midsection to his chest, to his neck, to his beard. She lifted her hand and placed it against his jaw.

He held himself completely still, afraid that if he so much as breathed he'd give away *everything*. Every moment he'd watched her a little too closely, wished she'd smile at him the way she smiled at Aiden, wished he didn't turn into some cardboard asshole the moment she glanced at him.

Basically, every moment he'd ever been a pathetic loser. He'd rather do a lot of shitty things than ever let anyone see that.

She leaned closer, her breasts very nearly brushing his chest, and he kept holding himself still, his arms locked, keeping her at a distance. Not a safe enough one, but a distance at least.

"You're very *tall*," she said earnestly.

"And you, honey, are very, very, *very* drunk."

She grinned and gave a little breathless laugh. "It's so *funny*." She rubbed her hand up and down his jaw as if she didn't have any idea what she was doing to him.

She doesn't, you fucking moron.

"Come on. In the truck." He led her around to the passenger side and opened the door for her, keeping his gaze averted as he placed his hand on the small of her back and gave her a little shove into the truck.

He closed the door and took a deep breath of the cold spring night, trying to get his head on straight and his brain functioning at some normal capacity because clearly he'd lost it somewhere along the way tonight.

Staying. Talking. Agreeing to things that involved spending more time in her presence.

Yeah, he had to get her home and pray for vodka-aided amnesia.

He climbed into the driver's side and shoved his key into the ignition. What a day. What a *problem*. But it was almost over. He just had to get her home.

He glanced over at her, sprawled in the passenger seat, eyes closed, hair a tangled red halo around her head.

"Buckle up."

She made a muffled sound, bringing her elbows into her sides and waving her forearms around. "Can't. T. rex arms." Then she laughed, uproariously, as she kept waving half her arms around and most decidedly not buckling her seat belt.

God was seriously testing him. He reached over and grabbed the seat belt, ignoring the fact that she was still laughing, her soft breath against his neck. He did his best to buckle her in, trying to ignore the fact he could feel her gaze on him.

"Did you know you have a dimple when you smile?" she asked softly.

His gaze locked onto hers, though he shouldn't have let it. Because his heart beat was unsteady, that usual too tight feeling invading his body.

"It was the first time I've ever seen it. In there." She poked at his cheek. "You could stand to smile more."

He sat back in his seat and looked out the windshield. "What's your address?" he muttered.

"The moon," she said, laughing uproariously again.

He narrowed his gaze at her. "A street name, and a number, honey."

She smiled over at him. "Why do you keep calling me honey?"

"I don't . . ." God, he needed to get away from her. "Just tell me your address."

"I don't think I remember."

"Give me your license."

She clutched her hands over her pockets, still grinning. "Never."

"Kayla."

"Just take me back to your place," she said with the wave of a hand. "I want to see your workshop."

"No."

She blinked over at him. "Well, I'm not telling you my address."

"Why the hell not?"

"Because I want to see your workshop," she replied as if it was the most logical thing in the world.

"Guess what, Kayla? Drunk women aren't cute," he returned irritably. Because the last thing he needed was her laughing and joking and talking about him having a dimple. It wasn't that he couldn't control himself—he wasn't a reprehensible ass. It was just . . .

Aiden wanted this woman, and the more Liam wanted her, the more this was going to suck balls. Because of course Kayla would want Aiden over him, and he was never going to put it to her as some kind of choice, so this was all futile torture.

"Guess what, Liam?" she returned, mimicking his voice. "Drunk or not—I don't care if I'm being cute for the enjoyment of men."

"Touché," he muttered, glancing over at her.

Her mouth was firmed into a line, her hands were crossed over her chest, and she looked at him—stubbornness etched into her every feature.

"You're not going to back down on this, are you?"

She smiled, her whole face softening. "Nope. Kayla Gallagher is *done* backing down."

He let out a long-suffering sigh. "To my workshop it is." Just another circle of hell to survive.

Chapter Four

Kayla sat in the passenger seat of Liam's truck quite proud of herself. Liam might think drunk Kayla was *not cute*, but she thought drunk Kayla was something of a genius. Drunk Kayla followed her instincts. Drunk Kayla was spontaneous. Drunk Kayla had figured out the next step in her life.

Do. Make. Create.

She wasn't going to be taken home and shuffled into her under-decorated apartment to be depressed about the turns her life had taken all over again. She was going to see Liam's workshop.

She'd never spent any time wondering what Liam did with his free time. Where he might live, what his friends might be like. She'd always considered him something of an imposing, irritable rock.

Only because he thinks you're fragile.

She scowled at the memory. She supposed it was nicer than him *hating* her, and there was a little curl of something like sympathy over him thinking he only knew how to fix things, but mostly she hated that he'd seen her as nothing but a breakable *thing*.

He was wrong. He had to be wrong. She'd stepped away from Gallagher's, hadn't she? That was no fragile feat. Not in that family.

"Well, we're here," Liam muttered gruffly.

Funny, a little meal with him and suddenly his gruff made her smile. She looked out the window. It was nearly dark, but she could see he'd parked on the street like many in the neighborhood.

Out the window was a little brick house, kind of gingerbread-like with a pointed eave over the door. The porch light was on, and she supposed Liam was the kind of guy who'd always remember to turn on his porch light if he went out at night.

The yard was neatly kept, with a little sidewalk up to the front door and a concrete pathway toward the back, from what she could tell in the dusky dark.

"I like it," Kayla offered.

"My life is complete," he said drily.

She smirked at him and pushed open the truck door. "Is your workshop inside?"

"No." He gave a gusty sigh and got out of the truck.

Kayla didn't wait around for him to round the truck or lead the way. She walked straight for his door, though the ground seemed strangely uneven and she couldn't quite seem to walk in a straight line.

Suddenly, his hand was gripping her arm, helping to keep her upright in a sea of swaying grass.

"For fuck's sake, you're going to break your neck."

She opened her mouth to tell him he was *wrong* and she was *fine*, but she stumbled a bit—surely over a hole—and had to hold on to Liam to keep herself from taking a header onto the sidewalk.

He was so very tall, and sturdy, like you could lean and lean and lean and he would never bend. The direct opposite of her, who bent and bent and bent until she snapped.

She frowned at the depressing thought, even as she leaned harder against him. He led her around the house to a patchy little backyard and what appeared to be a detached garage that faced an alley or street behind his house.

All the homes around were built in a similar fashion, separated by chain-link fences, but when Liam unlocked and pulled open his garage door, flicking on a light, she doubted any other houses in the neighborhood boasted *this*.

There was a big table across the far side, various machinery on it as well as hanging from shelves and corkboard across the walls. To the far corner there were stacks of wood and a little table full of paints and paintbrushes.

On the opposite side of that were shelves and boxes of what looked to be finished carvings or *child toys* or what have you. She started to move toward them, but his grip tightened on her arm.

Warm and strong. She looked curiously down at his fingers around the pretty purple and green pattern of her dress sleeve. Rough and scarred and fascinating, she thought she could look at his hands forever.

"You're not stumbling around my workshop, breaking my stuff or hurting yourself."

"I can walk," she replied, still staring at his long fingers curled around her arm.

"You've proven you *can't*," he replied.

She harrumphed, though she had to admit the floor in this room seemed a bit topsy-turvy too. "I want to see . . ." But she trailed off as her gaze landed on one of the tables.

He had rows and lines of tools meticulously organized. But sitting in the middle of one of the tables was a hunk of wood, as though started and left unfinished.

Which didn't seem like Liam at all.

"What's that?" she asked, pointing to the . . . It was a bear. Like the one she'd bought the other day. A grinning bear, she was nearly certain.

"I was working before my brother so rudely interrupted me."

His brother. Aiden. The one she was supposed to have had a drink with. She never would have gotten drunk with Aiden, she didn't think.

Odd. Why would she behave differently around them? They were from the same family. She'd known them both forever. But she couldn't imagine letting down her inhibitions with Aiden.

A few hours ago, she would have said the same for Liam, but here she was. Drunk and demanding.

She looked at the half-finished figure, then back at him. "It's a bear."

"Yes," he replied, his grip on her arm loosening, his entire body almost leaning away from her. Interesting reaction, though she couldn't quite figure out why. It felt almost as though the points in her brain wouldn't connect. Some thoughts were stuck on one side; some observations were stuck on the other. None could bridge the gap to make sense.

"I want to touch it."

He made an odd noise, maybe a squeak, if it had come out of a woman, but everything about his voice was so low and gravelly, nothing could quite be considered a squeak from him.

Still, he led her closer, and though his grip had loosened it was still *there*. Strong and sure, and she had no doubt that if she tripped or fell or, well, passed out—as seemed a little possible with the way her head was spinning—Liam would catch her. Keep her upright and safe.

Yes, she was very, very drunk. Still, she reached out for the half-formed bear and grabbed it. It fit into her palm, and unlike the one she'd bought the other day, this one was rough. It had most of the carving done, but it hadn't been polished.

"It needs a mouth," she said, running her finger over its face, surprised at the rough texture compared to the smooth gloss on the mouth of her figurine.

"I hadn't decided on the expression yet."

"It matches mine, except it has overalls instead of a dress. So it should be smiling. Grinning. Happy, naturally."

"Maybe it should be scowling," he muttered.

"No," she argued. "They're a couple. They should be happy. They match." She glanced up at him, surprised to find him awfully close. His features seemed a little wavy, but his eyes were that unnatural, piercing blue.

And there was something in them, something she should recognize. Not just his usual gruff stiffness, but something . . . else.

She blinked, then squinted, staring hard and trying to put it together.

"Fine. It'll be smiling. Happy?" He tried to move, maybe away from her, but she only sort of swayed with him. He was holding her arm after all.

"Can I have it?" she asked, curling her fingers around it. She didn't know how to explain the desire to keep it, but she didn't want to put it back down.

Something in his jaw tensed, and he gave an oddly stiff nod. "Fine. When it's done, it's yours."

"Do I have to pay for it?"

His eyebrows drew together. "Are you, Kayla *Gallagher*, trying to stiff me out of more money this evening?"

He drew out her last name like the curse that it was, cutting through some of that dizzying buzz, leaving only a kind of vague nausea. But his blue eyes, so dang blue, were steady on hers, and his stare was just like his hand on her arm, a steadying, *solid* thing holding her up.

"My grandmother cut me off," she said, not sure why, and it even sounded a little slurred to her ears.

His usually impassive—or grumpy—face widened then, shock, clear as day. "I'm . . . sorry."

Her head fell back in an attempt to look him better in the eye, those perfect blue *steady* points of strength. "Funny, you're the only one who's said that to me."

His eyebrows drew together, his lips softening into something almost like sympathy. Sympathy for her, Kayla Gallagher, who'd had so much handed to her and not been the least bit grateful for it.

But she didn't want to think about gratefulness or Gallagher's or being cut off. She wanted to think about how Liam's lips looked when they weren't pressed together in a firm, disapproving line.

He had a nice mouth. It very nearly looked soft. As though she could press her lips to his and not be met by smooth, immovable rock.

What would it be like to kiss Liam Patrick? A few hours ago she might have laughed hysterically at the question, but in the warm glow of his workshop, his mouth up close and surprisingly tempting, she found herself wondering.

Kayla Gallagher was staring at his mouth, an almost considering expression on her face.

A very drunk Kayla Gallagher, he reminded himself quickly. Sober Kayla wouldn't consider a thing on his face if he asked her to, and it was important to not let his idiot brain think otherwise.

Clearly the woman was having a little quarter-life crisis of sorts. She'd been cut off by her grandmother, had been stood up by her date, and had wanted nothing more than to get drunk in a bar and see his workshop.

Kayla Gallagher was a *mess*.

And not yours to fix.

He'd do well to remember that. All he had to do was keep his mouth shut, let her look around, and then take her home. She was not his responsibility or his problem.

"Do you want to talk about it?" Because, really, when had he ever let ownership keep him from trying to fix a problem?

Her blue eyes stared up at his as if he were some mythical creature. Well, she was drunk enough she was probably seeing two of him. *That* was the reasonable explanation.

"I just had to get out, you know?" she said, her voice something like a hushed whisper.

"Well, no." *Out* was not a word in his vocabulary. Especially when it came to his family or the family business.

"I was suffocating. Which sounds dramatic, but I felt it. Like I couldn't breathe. Like someone was pressing me down into this lifeless, colorless, *pointless* decoration." She pressed her hand to his chest, her arm shifting in the circle of his fingers, her warm palm pushing lightly against him. As if she could demonstrate.

"You could never be pointless, Kayla." Which was also something he shouldn't have said, but Kayla had been something like fresh air in all those years of answering to Gallaghers. She was quiet, yes, definitely a little skittish, but she was kind. Always kind in the midst of orders expected to be followed to the letter.

Yes, she'd seemed fragile compared to her iron maiden of a grandmother and her slick, formidable businessman of an uncle who'd run Gallagher's for so long. Her father, who ran the place now, reminded Liam of ice—cold, sharp, brutal if you let it be. Then there'd been Dinah, Kayla's cousin—a pretty package, but with the grandmother's steel underneath it all.

Kayla was none of those things. Soft and warm, scared and timid. So maybe it made sense she felt like she'd been suffocating in that family. Pressed down into the background.

"Why do you keep touching me?" he asked, when she said nothing else. When she simply stood there with her hand on him. He couldn't seem to escape it. Her body pressed to his, leaning against his, brushing against his, and now her hand over his heart.

She's drunk, you idiot, all the reason there is.

"I don't know," she said, as if arguing with the harsh words his mind was trying to tell him. "It's kind of fascinating to think of you as something real and breathing instead of a vaguely disapproving statue." She looked at her hand on his chest, and no matter how he tried to breathe like a normal person and not someone who'd just run a marathon, he could see her hand move with the rise and fall of his chest.

He still had his fingers curled around her arm, in an effort to keep her from crashing into things in his workshop. In an effort to keep her upright and unharmed.

Why did that have to feel like his responsibility?

Maybe because he was so focused on *not* being focused on her hand on him, he missed that she'd moved her other arm until she traced her fingers across the whiskers on his jaw.

He nearly jerked away, holding himself still only because if he jerked, he'd jerk her with him.

"I remember when you didn't have a beard," she said, staring at his chin.

"I remember when you had braces," he replied, and though he wasn't drunk, he felt a little off. All this close quarters and her and . . .

Her dark blue eyes rose to his. "Did you pay that close of attention?"

Always. "No. I just figure if we're pointing out how people have changed . . ."

"I'm trying to change," she said, her eyebrows drawing together.

"Why would you want to change?"

"Because I don't like myself very much. I haven't been happy much, and I kept waiting for something to change—something big to happen that would suddenly reveal itself to me as the thing I needed to do. But . . . it's not coming. It's never coming."

She sounded so bleak, and it wasn't something Kayla Gallagher should feel. She was beautiful and bright, and though she'd been cut off, she was a part of this privileged world. She could have been anything, done anything.

Before he could offer something comforting or sage in response, she straightened her shoulders, her hands leaving his body, though he was ashamed to realize he'd moved a little toward her as she'd pulled her hand away, as if he could keep that physical connection longer.

Yeah, he really needed to be avoiding physical connection, or connection of any kind.

"So I decided to stop waiting and start doing." She gave a sharp nod and looked around his workshop. "You do, all the time. You do and you make and *I* want to do something like that. I can paint—did you know that?"

He shook his head vaguely because she looked so determined and very nearly fierce, this woman he'd always viewed as fragile.

"I always liked to. I even thought about going into art. Graphic design or similar to make it practical, but . . ."

"But what?"

She chewed on her bottom lip, so he forced his gaze to her hairline, where the rich red strands curled around her face.

"I was afraid. I've always been afraid. Of being a failure, or not being good enough. I was always afraid of letting someone down, of letting Gallagher's down, because Gallagher's is all that matters really. It's all that ever mattered."

She blinked, and he didn't think she so much looked at him as she did *through* him while her mind was somewhere else.

"I should get drunk all the time. I'm figuring all sorts of shit out," she said with a little laugh. "Because that's it, I've been afraid. And I'm not going to be anymore. *That's* what I'm going to change."

"Well, I suppose that's a, uh, good, um, choice," Liam offered lamely. She didn't need him fixing things at all. She had it all figured out. Which was good, really. Great, in fact. Get her home and she'd no longer be his problem.

She pressed her hand to her stomach, the smile on her face dimming to something more like a grimace. "Well, I'm not ready to give up fear quite yet, because right now I'm very afraid I'm going to throw up."

Well, shit.

Chapter Five

When Kayla opened her eyes the next morning, she immediately closed them again. Everything in her vision had wavered and rolled, so it seemed safer to keep her eyes shut.

Except she still felt like she was rolling or spinning or something. Why had she insisted on getting so drunk? What had she been trying to prove? The morning-after misery was never, ever worth it.

She'd had a few hangovers in her day, but usually from just one extra glass of wine. And she'd always woken up in her own bed. Not someone else's.

Oh God, she was in someone else's bed. She thought back to the night before, pressing the back of her hand to her forehead and hoping it might stop the evil pounding.

She'd been going on a date with Aiden, except . . . Liam had shown up, hence the drinking, and she'd . . .

Her memory got a little blurry beyond that, like a dirty lens had been put over everything that happened. There'd been, well, drinking obviously. Something in a truck, a bear.

Puking. There had definitely been throwing up in the grass of Liam's little backyard. Which was horrifying enough, but remembering the fact she'd thrown up in Liam's yard meant remembering she'd *insisted* on him taking her to his workshop, which was at his house.

She was in a strange room. Presumably in a strange house. Surely she wasn't in Liam Patrick's bed. Surely . . .

She opened one eye, taking in her surroundings. She was in a bed. A very masculine bed. Dark linens. One pillow.

She closed her eyes again, trying to breathe through both nausea and panic. Okay, so she'd made some poor choices last night, but the bright side was she'd done it in front of someone who didn't matter.

Something in her chest shifted painfully at that, but she couldn't put enough pieces of last night together to figure out why it settled all wrong. What could have happened last night that would make her think he mattered?

She opened her eyes and pushed herself into a sitting position, quickly scanning the room, but Liam wasn't there. She seemed to have been the only one who had slept in the bed last night, and . . .

She was not wearing the dress she'd been wearing last night.

Oh shit. Oh shit, shit, shit, *shit*. What on earth had she been thinking last night? She should have gone home the second Liam showed up with Aiden's lame in-person-by-his-brother brush-off. Instead she'd gotten drunk and . . .

She didn't remember anything inside this bedroom. She certainly didn't remember sex, or Liam naked. Naked. Oh God, Liam naked, and she didn't even remember. Had he touched her? Was he a good kisser?

She shook her head, but that only made it pound harder.

What a failure.

She rubbed her temples, something about failure poking at her sore brain. She had to get out of here. She had to go home and try to forget this night. Surely Liam wouldn't be any more eager to remember it.

On less than steady legs, she pushed out of bed. *Liam Patrick's bed,* an annoying voice whispered in her mind. She placed a palm on either side of her head and pushed, hoping to steady the swirling dizziness.

After a few moments, some of it dissipated. She looked down at her legs. They were bare. Completely. She was wearing a T-shirt, not hers, and zero underwear. She smelled vaguely of men's soap.

A wave of nausea rolled through her, but she forced herself to breathe through it as she grabbed one of the blankets off the bed and wrapped it around herself.

She needed clothes, and her purse, and her shoes, and then she needed to disappear. She edged toward the door in the small room, hoping her roiling stomach would behave.

Another deep breath, a desperate attempt to marshal some courage—

a thing she wasn't very used to at all. It had taken courage to quit Gallagher's, but then she'd spent the past six months recovering from it—a whiny, sniveling baby, really.

This sort of rock-bottom moment showed her how clearly she'd been an idiot. Waiting around, feeling sorry for herself, moving through life as if she'd been personally victimized.

If anything good was going to come out of this failure, then she had to decide to make some good come out of it. She lifted her head as much as her aching brain would let her and sailed down the hall hoping to find Liam sooner rather than later.

She reached the end of the hall and stepped into a warmly lit, if spartan, living room. And there was Liam. He was sitting in an awfully uncomfortable-looking chair, phone cradled to his ear, while his hands held a small piece of wood and a knife. He murmured into the phone and scraped the blade across the piece of wood, and Kayla squinted at it trying to make out its shape.

But he suddenly dropped the wood, and the phone, and the knife, as he jumped to his feet, swearing as he sucked his finger into his mouth.

"I didn't mean to startle you," she offered.

"No. Um . . . Hold on." He grabbed the phone that had clattered to the floor, saying something into the speaker before hitting end.

He faced her, eyes wide, discomfort written all over his face. Maybe she was doing this drunken-hookup thing all wrong. Maybe there was a protocol she was failing at?

She cleared her throat, holding the blanket tightly at her chin. Something from last night filtered back to her. Something about not being afraid anymore, and that seemed right. Yes, she had made a mistake, she'd failed, but now it was time to own up to it and deal with the consequences.

She wasn't going to be *afraid* anymore. She wouldn't let anyone put her in that shrinking spot, including herself. "I should apologize."

"No, it's—"

"I was drunk and I can't imagine how annoying. And you were kind enough to bring me here and . . ." She clutched the blanket tighter. "Well, I don't remember exactly what happened, but I appear to be practically naked, so."

Liam made something like a choking sound. "We didn't . . ." He cleared his throat. "You just had vomit all over your dress. You . . .

you . . . I mean, we, uh . . . came inside and you took a shower and I, uh . . . washed your dress. You were . . . You did it yourself, that is. I wasn't involved in the . . ." He swallowed. "I had to help a little with the T-shirt, but, um, I mean, I didn't . . ."

"So we didn't sleep together?"

"Oh God, no. No. No."

"Well, you don't have to be *that* emphatic," she muttered, feeling foolish that his flat and horrified denial poked at her pride.

"You puked all over my bushes."

She squeezed her eyes shut, trying to fight off the embarrassment with bravery, but it seemed to be impossible. She could feel the hot flush creep up her neck and into her cheeks. She was probably as red as a tomato.

"It happens to the best of us," he said as if trying to make her feel better. "I just meant, it's not really the best foreplay."

Something about Liam Patrick saying "foreplay" did nothing to erase the heat in her cheeks. She forced herself to open her eyes, forced herself to be brave. "I am sorry for all the trouble I must have put you through."

His mouth curved a little at that, a nonverbal acceptance of her apology. But something about his mouth tugged at a memory. Something about . . . soft lips? "Did we . . . kiss?" she asked, against her better judgment. "I mean, before the puking."

"No. No, definitely not."

"Are you sure? Because . . ." He raised an eyebrow at her and she wilted. Okay, so apparently kissing her was his worst nightmare. But she remembered . . . something. Or had she dreamed it?

"Because what?"

She sighed, pressing a hand to her temple as she held the blanket to her chest with the other. "Can I have my clothes? I want to go home."

"Of course. Follow me." He picked up his knife and wood and set it on an end table she wondered if he'd made himself. Again, she squinted at the wood, but she couldn't make out the shape.

So she turned, following him back to the hallway, the blanket trailing behind her. It reminded her of playing queens and princesses with Dinah when they were little girls, which reminded her of Gallagher's, which somehow reminded her of how she'd gotten here.

Liam led her to a little mudroom that was filled almost completely by a washer and dryer. He leaned down to pull her clothes out of the dryer. She tried not to wince. Her dress was probably ruined if he'd put it through the machine.

Still, it was a small price to pay.

Don't be a coward, Kayla. Be brave. Go after what you want. She'd wanted to be a princess as a little girl, or a queen, but mostly she'd pretended to be the lady's maid while Dinah had been the leader. But Kayla had always secretly wished a handsome prince would sweep her off her feet.

Liam handed over her rumpled clothes. She took them, caught in that piercing blue gaze. He had never been the prince in her imagination. Any flittering thoughts to the contrary were clearly her hangover talking.

She'd only ever had a crush on *Aiden*. She was supposed to have gone out with *Aiden*. Maybe Liam wasn't quite as dour as she'd always thought him, but that didn't change what she was after.

"Can you, uh, not tell your brother?" she asked, not sure why her chest contracted painfully at the words.

Something moved through his expression, an emotion Kayla didn't know how to analyze, but he gave a sharp nod.

"Consider it our secret."

Liam loaded his toolbox and tool belt into the back of his truck. He'd told Kayla to meet him out here once she was dressed and ready to go. He'd drive her home and that would be that.

There was a simmering kind of frustration building inside of him and he wished he could spend a couple hours quietly in his workshop getting something accomplished. Then maybe he could figure it out and eradicate it.

Instead, he had to go to a few appointments with Dad, and often that work could relax him too. But he didn't feel like being around anyone right now, no matter how much he enjoyed his father's company.

He wanted to be alone. He wanted to sort out these unwanted and unbidden *feelings* assaulting him. He was not a big *feelings* guy. He did what had to be done. He fixed.

He did not get bent out of shape about being asked to keep something from his brother. He hadn't even been planning on telling

Aiden. So why it grated that Kayla had asked him not to say anything about her drunken evening chastely in his bed, Liam couldn't figure out.

He shouldn't be surprised. Of course she didn't want Aiden to know. Even though nothing had happened, it didn't exactly look good on either of them that she'd gotten drunk and Liam had taken her home.

He slammed the truck bed door closed. He was probably as irritated with himself as he was with everyone else, and he didn't get it.

He wasn't sure he wanted to. But it was a problem, and problems always needed fixing. Quite the conundrum.

He glanced up at his house and Kayla stepped out of his door. She held her shoes in one hand, her colorful purse strapped across her chest. She was wearing the dress he'd washed for her, but he puzzled over the fact she was wearing his T-shirt over it.

She approached and though she was always pale, the hangover paleness of her skin seemed to make her freckles stand out even more. Despite clearly looking sick, she was pretty. Clean and fresh, and a little disheveled.

"Sorry. My dress kind of, um, shrunk in the wash and . . ." She made a gesture with her hands that he had the uncomfortable feeling had to do with her breasts, so he just nodded his head.

"It's fine. Keep it."

"Oh, well, I can always return it."

Liam shrugged. He didn't expect to be seeing Kayla much after this. If she didn't remember taking a shower after throwing up in his yard, he doubted she remembered her grand plans to have him teach her woodworking.

Which was good. Great, even. He didn't have time to teach anyone shit.

"Ready?" he asked, maybe something more of a demand, as he rounded the truck to the driver's side. He hopped in and waited for her to do the same.

But she stood outside the passenger door, an odd expression on her face. Eventually though, she clambered into the passenger side seat.

He shoved the key into the ignition and turned it. He felt exactly as he always felt around Kayla. Uncomfortable and stiff. Whatever camaraderie they'd had last night had clearly worn off. Maybe that had been some sort of bizarre effect of her drinking. He felt comfortable enough to let down some of his guard.

It was certainly all back today. He was a damn fortress.

"What's your address?"

She rattled off the number and street, clutching her purse in her lap. She looked as uncomfortable as he felt and he realized part of it was probably the nasty hangover she must have. He should've offered her some breakfast or some coffee. He should . . . not be a dick. It wasn't her fault this was weird.

Okay, it was kind of her fault that it was weird, but sometimes when people were in complex situations in their lives, they made mistakes. She was young. Three whole years younger than he was.

He'd made dumb mistakes. Somewhere along the line. Probably.

Still, the point was people made mistakes and Kayla was going through a rough personal time. Maybe he didn't understand it and maybe she'd had a lot of stuff handed to her due to her family's wealth or whatever, but that didn't mean it wasn't still a tough time for her.

So he needed to stop being Fortress Patrick, or Captain Stick in the Ass as Aiden might say, and *do* something about it. *Fix it.*

"You want to stop at McDonald's or something? Sometimes greasy food helps a hangover a little bit."

She still didn't look at him, but she pressed her hands to her stomach. "I can't decide if the idea is revolting or absolutely what I need, but you don't have to do that. I've already imposed on you enough."

"It's not an imposition to go through the drive-through at McDonald's on the way to drop you off. Besides, my first appointment this morning is kind of near your place." If the opposite direction was kind of.

"Kind of," she repeated, her mouth curving a little. "You are not quite what I thought you were, Liam. You're . . ."

When she didn't finish her sentence, he knew he should let it go. But there were a lot of things he knew when it came to Kayla Gallagher, and in the past twenty-four hours he seemed to ignore all of them. "I'm what?" he asked, flicking his glance to her as he drove.

Her mouth curved even more. "You've always had a very standoffish demeanor when it comes to me. But that's not actually you at all, is it?"

He returned his gaze to the road, not sure he had it in him to meet her all-too-seeing expression. Outside of customers, whom he made an effort to charm, most people assumed he was a serious and standoffish guy. He'd never thought much of that perception. He didn't care if people saw him that way, because it wasn't who he was. It was his persona or his shell or something. It had nothing to do with him as a man.

"I like to fix things. I like to help people. It's all the same really. Standoffish or not, it's not . . ." He shook his head. Was he trying to get into some deep philosophical conversation with her? No. "I don't mind helping. End of story."

"I see that. It's a very admirable quality the way you do it."

"The way *I* do it?"

"Yes, there's a difference between wanting to help people, to fix something, and wanting to control via fixing or helping them. You help to fix a situation, or jump in to lend someone a hand. Some people . . . well, they lend a hand because they want to use their hand to shape you."

He shot her another quick glance and he figured she was thinking about her family. The Gallaghers had always been something of an enigma to Liam. He'd had more than one conversation with his father about how strange the Gallagher family was. Because for as many weird family issues as the Patricks had, there was a very clear bond, a connecting tissue of love.

Liam didn't always know how to get along with his brother, or how not to be a little bit bitter, but he still loved Aiden. He'd do anything for him or Mom or Dad.

He didn't understand people who would shape someone into what they wanted them to be. Who would . . . what was the word she'd used last night? Suffocate. She'd felt suffocated and pressed down into decoration, and he didn't get it. But it didn't surprise him in the least the Gallaghers could and did.

He pulled into the McDonald's lot and glanced at Kayla. She had both hands pressed to her stomach now, a miserable look on her face.

She leaned over the console between them and placed her hand on his forearm. Her pinky brushed the bare part of his wrist where the cuff of his shirt ended.

He had the uncomfortable memory of helping her put that T-shirt on last night. He'd done his best to keep his eyes averted, and she *had* pulled the shirt over her body, she'd just been struggling to get her arms in the sleeves.

So he'd had to look at least a little, and there'd been acres of pale skin and light-reddish freckles just about everywhere. He'd been as respectful and responsible as possible, but he couldn't erase the memory of how her red hair looked wet and tangled, or how her skin smelled with his soap on it.

"I can't bear the thought of you putting yourself out anymore for me, so please just get me an order of hash browns and maybe a hot chocolate in the drive-through. Then you'll take me home and I will get out of your hair. Because you have done so much more than enough." She squeezed his arm, the pressure warm and sure. "Please."

He inclined his head in agreement. Honestly, the best thing for both of them was to get this over with. No memories of freckles or tangled hair to haunt him.

Okay, it'd probably still haunt him, but she wouldn't be all . . . there watching it happen.

He drove to the drive-through and ordered her breakfast. He ordered himself a coffee and then drove to the address she'd given him.

Any time he glanced over at her, no matter how hard he tried not to, she had her eyes closed. Clearly she was still dealing with some nausea or dizziness, but she nibbled on the hash brown and drank the hot chocolate and somehow looked all too appealing doing it in the passenger seat of his truck.

He pulled up to her address and frowned at the nondescript apartment building. "This is where you live?" It wasn't that it was particularly terrible, but it was bland and very close to dingy.

She opened her eyes and looked at the building and grimaced. "Yes. This is where I live."

"I can't picture you living in a place like this." Which was another one of those things he should have kept to himself. What the hell was wrong with him?

She glanced over at him, cocking her head. "Why?"

"I . . . You're just . . . You know, I don't know."

Her mouth curved into a full-blown smile. "Yes, you do. Why are you surprised I live here?"

He sighed. This woman. "I just figured you'd live in some sort of hipster place with gardens and shit."

She laughed and then pressed a hand to her temple because it clearly aggravated her hangover. "I used to. But I don't have the funds for hipster garden shit anymore."

"Right. Well."

She gathered up her trash, and he tried to tell her to leave it, but she shook her head.

"I'm not leaving any more mess in your life. I promise." She smiled at him as she pulled the keys out of her cross-body purse. "Thank you. I can't even begin to express how much I appreciate everything you did."

"Even shrinking your dress?" he asked, nodding to his T-shirt over her clothes.

"You were patient and kind, and you let me puke in your bushes and sleep in your bed. I think a shrunken dress was a very small price to pay."

"Well, sure." He should let her go. He shouldn't say anything more. Clearly she didn't remember any of the stuff they'd talked about last night, or at least most of it. He should let all of that go and let this be the last time he saw Kayla Gallagher for a very long time.

"Did you still want those lessons?"

She stopped in the middle of pushing the car door open. "Lessons?"

Why was he an idiot?

"Oh right," she said, her face brightening. "I wanted you to teach me how to carve something. And you're going to make me a bear. I remember that now. I wanted to make something." She held the crumpled trash in one hand and her keys in the other and stared at him with an all too alluring smile gracing her features. "Will you let me paint the bear?"

"Because you used to like to paint," he replied lamely.

"I haven't done that in the longest, longest time," she said, her voice very nearly far away before she shook her head, then grimaced at the action.

"You're . . . uh . . . welcome whenever. I work every night in the workshop unless I get a call. I mean you'll probably be busy. I'm sure Aiden will reschedule."

"Aiden. Right." Her lips pressed together, and she looked like a very stern teacher for a second. But only a second and then her face was all bright smiles again. "That doesn't mean we can't be friends, right?"

"Friends." She wanted to be his friend. She looked damn near hopeful. Which he didn't understand at all, because why the hell would someone sweet and bright want to be friends with him? They had nothing in common. They hadn't even liked each other up until last night.

"But it's fine if you don't want to," she said in a rush. "I crashed into your life enough. I don't want to be forcing myself on you."

"You're not forcing yourself on me. Here." He shifted so he could pull one of his cards out of his wallet. "That's got my cell number on it. If you ever want to paint or woodwork, just text or call. If you don't, no hard feelings and you can pick up your bear at the farmers' market in probably two weeks."

She took the offered card and looked at it curiously. "You give all your customers your cell phone number?"

"Well, Dad refuses to carry a cell phone, and sometimes customers have emergencies late at night. It makes sense."

The curious look on her face didn't change as she looked from the card to his face and then back to the card. "Well, thank you. I'll probably call you then. As long as it's really okay."

"Really. In fact, painting is the part I hate the most, so I don't do much of it unless I think a piece really needs it. You can help."

She blinked as she slipped the card into her purse. "Help, huh?"

"Sure. Make, do, create, right?"

"You're not quite what I thought you were, Liam Patrick," she said softly. And then she did the strangest thing. She leaned over and brushed a kiss across his cheek. "You're a very good guy," she said, and then she was out of his truck before he could say another word.

Chapter Six

Kayla spent the next two days deleting all her temporary work profiles, determined to be done with temporary.

She had left Gallagher's because she didn't want that life. As much as she'd enjoyed her role as sustainability manager, it had been something Dinah had suggested. It hadn't been her own choice.

She needed to start making her own decisions, and she needed to start thinking about permanence. About *creating* her life.

So she scoured every online job site and applied for anything that sounded remotely appealing, even if she wasn't qualified.

Sometimes she'd catch herself staring at Liam's card that she'd put on her fridge with one of her kitten-shaped magnets. She'd avoided calling him because she felt bad for everything he'd had to do for her that night, but the more she made decisions about permanence and moving forward, the more having a hobby seemed like a good idea.

A new job. A new hobby. A new *life.* Maybe he'd let her paint some of his carvings. It would be something artistic and fun to spend a few hours a week doing.

The surprising thing of the whole Liam debacle had been that, from what she could remember, he'd actually been really easy to talk to. The more she thought about what she'd said to him before getting out of his truck that morning, the more she was convinced he absolutely was one of the most decent men she knew.

Maybe he had some sort of secret, horrible fetish, or was mean to his customers. Maybe he liked to kick puppies or eat peas. She didn't know. But a man who was eager to help just because he could fix things . . .

She didn't know anyone like that. It was downright fascinating.

When her phone rang she was jolted out of her Liam reverie. The screen read *Dinah.* Kayla bit her lip. She'd been avoiding Dinah for months, saying as little as possible the few times they'd accidentally run into each other.

But if she was striving to be brave, and to find permanence, and to create a life, then she couldn't be afraid to own up to some of the things she'd had to leave behind.

She accepted the call before she had a chance to talk herself out of it. "Hi, Dinah."

"Kay, I . . . I didn't expect you to actually answer."

Kayla acknowledged the familiar pain in her chest. She'd missed Dinah, the woman who'd been her best friend her entire life. It had been a necessary break, but that hadn't meant it had been an easy one.

"Well, I . . . I thought it might be important." She wasn't quite ready to spill her guts to Dinah. She needed a little more clarity before she got that far.

"It isn't, not really," Dinah replied. "But since I actually reached you, I'm going to ask anyway. I wanted to see if you'd please consider coming to my birthday dinner next week."

"Your birthday," Kayla repeated lamely. She'd spent her own birthday alone last month. Dinah had called, but Kayla hadn't answered. Dinah had sent flowers, and she'd been the only one. Even Grandmother's usual impersonal card had never appeared.

"Carter wants to make me dinner and told me to invite people, but you're the only one I'd want to invite besides him, and you don't have to give me a gift, because your presence would be my present. Really."

"Dinah—"

"No, don't answer right away, please. Think about it. Let the guilt really set in. I miss you."

Kayla's heart clenched uncomfortably. Dinah wasn't one to easily talk about emotions, nor did she usually ask Kayla to think things over or through. Usually she insisted, no matter how kindly.

"I'll think about it," Kayla returned, and she planned to. Very carefully. Because she still loved Dinah, still wanted to be friends, but she also didn't want to be flattened again by the Gallagher bulldozer.

"And just so you know, it's a Gallagher's-free zone," Dinah offered as though reading her mind. "It's just a dinner with my friends, otherwise known as you. Nothing business related. I promise."

"That doesn't sound much like you, Dinah," Kayla said carefully. Dinah had been convinced Gallagher's was her heart and soul and all that mattered not all that long ago.

"Things are different. I wish you'd give me a chance to prove that to you. I thought when I turned Grandmother's director of operations offer down, you'd see that."

"It isn't you. It's me."

Dinah laughed, somewhat bitterly. "You keep saying that, but I'm still the one you're not talking to."

"I'm not talking to Grandmother or my father either, if it helps." Not that they'd tried to talk to her. They'd considered her quitting a grand betrayal, one she should be punished harshly for.

"It doesn't and you know that," Dinah replied with none of their past humor about the situation of strained relations with the elder Gallaghers.

"Dinah, I don't want to be bulldozed anymore."

"Then don't. Come to dinner, and if I start talking Gallagher's, you have my permission to walk the hell out. Or smack me. Something. You don't *have* to sit there and take it."

Kayla opened her mouth to argue, but Dinah was already continuing on.

"Actually, screw that. You don't need my permission to walk out because it's your life and you get to do whatever you want. I'm just asking to spend my birthday with my best friend, and if you say no, I'll let it be. But I wasn't going to not ask."

"I'll think about it," Kayla said meekly, then frowned at that note in her voice. This wasn't about what Dinah wanted. It was about what *she* wanted to do. And it wasn't . . . It wasn't like Dinah was trying to *do* something to her. She was trying to repair a friendship.

Maybe, just maybe, one Kayla had been at fault for ruining. She'd blamed Dinah's hardheaded obsession with Gallagher's deep down, but maybe it was as simple as the fact that Kayla had *taken* it.

She'd never said no or walked away or stood up for herself. She'd cowered and let herself be swept along.

"Actually, I don't need to think about it. I'll come. I'll be there."

And if Dinah tried to bulldoze her, she wouldn't run away, and she wouldn't lay down so it could flatten her so easily. She would be brave, damn it.

"Friday then, at six. Carter's—well, our house."

Kayla might have spent a lot of time away from Dinah the last few months, but she still knew her cousin. She knew she was excited.

"Dinah . . . Are you happy with him?" Kayla asked. Although she felt timid prying into Dinah's love life, she was curious. And she was going to be brave in all things.

"I've never been happier," Dinah replied earnestly.

"Even . . . Even though you aren't director of operations at Gallagher's?"

"Yeah, I mean, it'd be nice because your dad's decisions leave a lot to be desired, but it's not the everything I thought it was. Not the position anyway and it's amazing to love someone and not have it be . . . conditional, I guess. Everything at Gallagher's tends to feel rather conditional."

"Yeah. It does." She'd always thought that said something about her, but maybe it wasn't about her at all. Maybe it was the way things were, and she needed to build her life regardless.

"Can I bring anything?" Kayla asked, more determined than ever to repair her relationship with Dinah.

"Just your beautiful self, sweetheart."

"I'll be there," Kayla said firmly. "And for the record . . . I miss you too."

Dinah was quiet for a few seconds. "You know, we could hang out tonight if you're free."

Kayla glanced at her fridge and Liam's card. "I actually might have plans tonight, but what about tomorrow?"

"I'll bring the wine. You supply the brownies."

"Deal."

They said their goodbyes and Kayla stared at her phone. She typed a text to Liam and waited for his response as she thought over her conversation with Dinah and the uncomfortable question it produced.

Because if she grew a backbone and stood up to people when she didn't agree with them, would she really need to keep running from Gallagher's?

* * *

Liam was a fool. And a moron. A fucking idiot. But he got home from work and went through the shower. Usually, he ate dinner and went straight to his workshop in his work clothes grimy from fixing things.

Today, he put on a fresh pair of jeans and a T-shirt and brushed his hair—something he barely did on a good day.

He was being the most pathetic of all morons possible. And he couldn't quite stop himself.

He shouldn't be excited or nervous or fucking primping like a teenager, because Kayla coming over meant nothing at all. She wanted to create something and maybe be friends so no big deal. He could be friends with a woman he found attractive. Especially ones who clearly liked his brother.

His brother who had essentially disappeared for two days as far as Liam could tell. Which wasn't uncommon, but Aiden had been pretty dead set on Kayla that day of the farmers' market.

But he hadn't been home, and as far as Liam knew, hadn't contacted Kayla.

And what do you know?

Not a whole lot. Except that he was an idiot.

He raked his fingers through his hair, which probably ruined any attempt he'd made to brush it. Which was fine, because he was not worried about his appearance. He was *never* worried about his appearance.

He muttered a curse, but it was cut off halfway through by his doorbell. He closed his eyes and took a deep breath. *You will not be an idiot. You will not be an idiot.*

He opened the door and plastered his best customer-ready smile on his face. "Hey."

She wore jeans and a thermal shirt with little printed . . . he squinted to try and figure it out. Owls? Purple owls. Her hair was pulled back into a braid, wisps of escaped red waving around her face.

"Here, I brought you something," she offered, shoving a small tin at him. He took it, if only because he was afraid she'd jam it into his chest again if he didn't.

"You didn't have to—"

She waved a hand in an odd gesture, stepping inside as he moved out of the way. "It's just brownies. I made a double batch as a, you know, thank-you for . . ."

He raised his eyebrows at her and she blew out a breath. "I don't know. It's a lot easier to be brave about shoehorning yourself into someone's life via text."

"You're not shoehorning. It was an offer." Her nerves settled his, ever the fixer.

"Right. Well, I . . . My cousin's birthday is next week, actually, and I wanted to maybe buy something of yours and paint it for her, though I don't know much about painting wood. But you could maybe show me?" Her blue eyes were both hopeful and concerned, and it would take a far stronger man than him to ever turn down that look.

"I could definitely show you. Let me just put these down and then we'll head out to the workshop."

She gave a sharp nod and he walked away, placing the brownies on the kitchen counter and grabbing his keys. When he returned to her, she was standing next to his fireplace, examining the short row of pictures there.

She looked back at him somewhat sheepishly. "I didn't realize you had such a big family," she said, pointing at the picture of the Patrick family reunion from the year after Dad's heart attack when Grandma had made a big deal about everyone attending. Even Aiden had showed up from who knew where.

"Dad's got nine brothers and sisters, and most of them have five-plus kids, then half of them have started in." At her wide-eyed look, he shrugged. "Irish Catholic."

She smiled. "So are we."

"I haven't seen you at mass."

She narrowed her eyes, sizing him up. "You do not go to mass."

He shrugged. "Not every Sunday, but Grandma Patrick has guilt trips down to an art form. Even Aiden graces a pew far more than you'd think to give him credit for."

She laughed, the sound bright and sweet in his house, which was the strangest thing, really. It wasn't as though he never dated, but he usually didn't have women in his living room laughing about his church attendance.

"So, um, workshop?"

"Right. Yes. Let's do that," she said, clasping her hands together.

They walked out back and to his garage. He focused on unlocking the padlock and not staring at the rainbow polka dots on her flimsy tennis shoes as her feet shifted behind him.

He didn't get why she was nervous when she was the one who'd suggested this whole thing, but he supposed it was better than him feeling like the awkward one.

He pushed open the garage door and glanced at the sky when a roll of thunder sounded. Fat drops of rain started to fall and Kayla hurried inside. Lightning flashed in the sky.

"Better close up," Liam offered, pulling the garage door back down and then flipping on the lights.

Something about being in his workshop relaxed his whole being, even with Kayla there. Here, there was no problem he couldn't solve, no thing he couldn't create. He didn't have to worry about his family, or Patrick & Sons. It was just him and what he could make out of a piece of wood.

And Kayla Gallagher.

He cleared his throat, which thankfully the thunder rumbled over. "I've got some stock that's unpainted," he said, walking over to the cabinet that held the pieces he'd finished but hadn't painted or glossed yet. "You can pick something from there, or if you have an idea I might be able to make something in time."

She studied him for a second, tugging on one flaming strand of hair. "Why?"

"Why what?"

"Why would you make something for me?"

"This *is* a hobby, but I do make money off of it. Which means, I make things for people when they request it."

"Oh. Right." She blinked, but then stepped forward to peer into the cabinet.

"I do a lot of kitchen materials. Spoons, trays, and the like. Then the animals of course. The decorative spoons are my biggest seller right now with the whole lovespoon thing."

"Lovespoon thing?" she asked.

Liam felt a little stupid for bringing it up, but hell, it *was* his biggest seller. He walked over to where he kept his little tags and handed her one.

She took the tag and read it thoughtfully, her mouth slowly curving as she did. "A lovespoon is a traditional craft that was historically given to a young woman by her suitor. As it lost its practical use, people began to hang their lovespoons on the wall as a treasured decorative item. Perfect for wedding and anniversary gifts, or to decorate your kitchen with a spoonful of love." She looked up at him, her eyes laughing. "Liam Patrick, that is downright romantic."

No matter that a little curl of embarrassment seemed to flush his face hot, he couldn't stop himself from smiling back. "Romance *sells*, Kayla."

She gave a little wondering laugh. "Mercenary romance. Well, I can't say I disapprove. Can I see one?"

"Hmm." He looked around his workshop. "You know, I don't think I have any finished. I've got one in progress." That he'd put aside to make her bear. Which was not something he needed to tell her.

He went over to his lineup of in-progress works and picked up the spoon. "I've only got the spoon part done, but I've kind of outlined what I want to do with the top," he said, handing it to her.

She took the heavy piece of wood that only had the spoon carved out. She ran her colorfully painted fingertips over the lines he'd sketched out.

"My mom had one that was a family heirloom, so I studied up on them when I was a kid. The different symbols mean different things. A lot of them have these little keyholes to represent home and security. Then there's . . ." He stopped himself. "You don't want to hear me yammer on about this."

Her blue eyes met his gaze and she smiled. "Of course I do. It's so fascinating. What's the bell for?"

"Marriage."

She continued to ask him questions about the lovespoons, and eventually she convinced him to show her his website where he had pictures of past works. She exclaimed over everything like it was a revelation, and Liam didn't know what exactly to do with that.

Dad had always called his woodworking a nice hobby, but as it was mainly decorative, he'd had no interest. And though Liam had been inspired to go into this hobby by his mother's love for that old lovespoon that had been in her family for generations, she'd never cared much for a hobby that wasn't about helping people. Aiden, of course, had either ignored his interest or teased him relentlessly for it.

Liam *had* impressed a few women with his handy skills, but most hadn't taken an actual interest in how he worked. Kayla asked a million questions, and when she picked a little bird to give her cousin, she'd even asked questions about the type of paint he used.

He'd gotten her set up with the paints and brushes she'd need and surreptitiously watched as she studied the bird from all angles before she chose which color to use first.

A boom of thunder, a bolt of lightning, and then they were plunged into total darkness.

"Well, shit," Liam muttered, digging his phone out of his pocket and flipping on the flashlight feature. Kayla had done the same and crossed over to the little window that looked over his backyard.

Lightning flashed and the rain came down in hard sheets. Liam stepped next to her and winced a little at the potential damage. A flooded yard and basement. His roof was in good repair, but old, and his gutters hadn't been cleaned yet this spring.

Crap.

He glanced at Kayla who was staring at the window, her eyes a little wide. Maybe she didn't care for the dark.

"I have flashlights and candles in the house, but not much out here. We could make a run for it if you want."

She shrugged. "I don't mind waiting it out. Always kind of fascinating to watch what nature can do." She smiled, then glanced up at him. "This was fun even if I didn't get to start painting."

"You really think it's fun?" he asked. It wasn't that he didn't believe her. It was just he'd never met anyone who'd taken such a keen interest in this thing he loved to do.

"Of course. You're not so bad to hang out with," she said, a teasing curve to her mouth, which was just barely illuminated by their phones and the occasional flash of lightning.

She was always pretty as a picture, but there was something almost fairy-ish about her in the odd flickering light. Her red hair seemed redder; her blue eyes seemed to glow. He was tempted to reach out and touch a freckle, just to see if it would fall away like glitter.

A flash of lightning and an almost simultaneous crack of thunder had him jumping back and Kayla squeaking in surprise.

They both laughed a little breathlessly, but Liam didn't go back to his previous spot next to her at the window. This was all a little too tempting, and regardless of temptation, of actually *liking* Kayla, Aiden had made his intentions clear, and Liam didn't need any other awkward, bitter thing between him and his brother.

"I better make sure everything's unplugged so the electricity doesn't get overloaded when it comes back on."

"Oh, I'll help," she offered cheerfully. A *friendly* gesture, and nothing else. An interest in woodworking was not an interest in *him,* and he'd do well to remember it.

Chapter Seven

As the storm raged on around the little garage, and the power continued to not come back on, Kayla could only sneak little glimpses at Liam as he double-checked to make sure all of his machinery was unplugged.

There'd been a little moment at the window there, almost like . . . She had to be fooling herself thinking for even a second Liam had been looking at her in a considering kind of way. They'd had plenty of interaction in their lives and he'd never looked *consideringly* at her.

Of course, the Liam Patrick she'd thought she'd known was not *this* Liam Patrick. Very near artistic, no matter how masculine his materials were. Romantic, even if it was because lovespoons sold.

It wasn't as if she'd ever thought him hideous. The Patricks were a handsome lot. She'd just always been dazzled by Aiden because he paid attention to her.

Now Liam was paying attention to her and she was dazzled by him, and maybe the problem was not the Patrick men, but Kayla herself. What did it say about her if she was easily swayed into liking one or the other simply because they gave her a few minutes of their time?

She frowned. This whole figuring herself out thing was neither fun nor comfortable, but it was necessary. So maybe she should stop thinking about either Patrick brother as a possible romantic entanglement.

"We got them all," Liam announced, standing from the crouch he'd been in to check the last outlet.

She turned her phone to him, her light illuminating his face. He held up a hand to shield his eyes.

"Hey, careful where you point that thing. I feel like I'm in an interrogation room." He grinned. "No, officer, I swear I had nothing to do with the blackout."

Her stomach swooped, something a little giddy working through her, much against her will. She could order her brain to be sensible and careful, after all, but her body seemed to react of its own volition to Liam. Especially grinning, joking Liam.

She'd had no idea something like that existed, but it was easy to see he relaxed here in his workshop. Maybe he'd even relaxed around her because they'd spent some time together. *Or because he's seen you puke*. Well, that too. Maybe, when it all was said and done, Liam was just shy and all those years she'd thought he'd looked at her with disdain he'd just been uncomfortable.

"Well, I think painting may have to wait until another day. Last time the power went out it took them something like ten hours to get it back."

"Oh, okay."

"It does look like the rain stopped," he offered, peering out the window. "I, um, if you want to come inside, I have a book you might like to borrow."

"A book?"

"It's about lovespoons," he said, his gaze still on the window. "The origin and the symbols and all that. If you're interested, that is."

"Oh, that sounds great," she said, trying to stop herself from grinning stupidly. She found the concept of lovespoons fascinating, almost as fascinating as she found the man Liam was turning out to be.

He flicked a glance to her, and in the faint glow of their phones she couldn't read the expression on his face, but something in her stomach swooped again.

"Okay, let's go before it starts up again." He walked over to the garage door and pushed it up and over. The wind howled and the sky had an eerie tint to it, dark clouds making it seem almost midnight instead of seven or eight o'clock.

Liam pulled the garage door down and locked his padlock. "Don't think the storm is done yet, do—"

Before he could finish his sentence, the sound of rain pounded toward them and then it was upon them. A hard, relentless downpour soaking through her clothes and hair in a matter of seconds.

"Inside," Liam yelled above the din, taking her hand and leading her at a jog toward his house.

She followed, a laughter bubbling up from somewhere. Liam's hand was big and warm and rough, and her flimsy shoes splashed through the mud and puddles of his yard.

He hurried up the porch steps, but for a second Kayla stood in the rain, soaking in the cold downpour, listening to the roaring sounds of droplets on concrete. It smelled like spring, and spring was all about renewal. Rebirth.

Wasn't that what she was after? A new birth, a new Kayla? Or maybe not so much new as a bright colorful blossom from a brown, dull stalk that had been hiding in the underbrush, but no more.

No more.

"Are you coming?" Liam asked. He'd flipped on his porch light and he was bathed in a faint yellow glow in the middle of this dark world.

Thunder boomed and lightning flashed in the sky. The wind started blowing the rain harder into her face, and she thought she might remember this moment and this feeling for a very long time.

Still, she walked over to the porch and stepped up under the overhang of his house. Water dripped from every part of her body—hair, nose, fingertips. "You better not let me into your house. I'll drip everywhere."

"You're old hat at wearing my clothes at this point. We'll get you a towel and some dry clothes to change into." He stepped inside, tugging his shoes off and tossing them onto a rumpled rug in the entryway corner. There was a pair of scuffed work boots already haphazardly on top.

Kayla followed suit, pulling her shoes and socks off and placing them a little more neatly next to his.

"I'll grab you a towel," he offered. He crossed his darkened living room quickly, heading to the hallway she knew led to his room. She nearly squeaked when he lifted his shirt up as he rounded the corner, as though making a move to taking it off. She didn't realize she was leaning to keep a glance of his now bared retreating back until she bumped into the wall.

She righted herself, pressed a wet, chilled hand to her hot cheek. Okay, so if she was operating under New Blossom Law, then maybe she said something about the shirtlessness. And wanting to see it. Maybe she went ahead and kissed him or said something outrageous.

Yes, she would do any or all of those things.

Except when he returned, towel and a bundle of clothes in hand, a camping lantern in the other, she could only manage an odd squeaking noise.

If he noticed, he didn't say anything about it. He simply put the clothes and lantern down on a little end table and handed her a towel. "Here. Dry yourself off, then help yourself to the bathroom to change. Let me know if you need anything else. Do you want something hot to drink? I think I have hot chocolate mix around here somewhere."

"You are full of surprises," she murmured, rubbing the towel over her face and hair.

"Are you insinuating a single man in his early thirties shouldn't have a chocolate beverage mix in his pantry?"

She couldn't stop herself from grinning stupidly at him. "Everyone should have a chocolate beverage mix in their pantry, Liam. But few men realize it, I think," she said as faux seriously as she could manage.

"I'll have you know, hot chocolate can be very manly," he returned, crossing his arms over his chest. She remembered suddenly and out of the blue watching him fix a sink in the Gallagher's kitchen once. She'd been transfixed by his muscled, working arms.

But then Aiden had swept in and told her an outrageous joke and she'd forgotten all about Liam's arms.

How, she wasn't quite sure. Maybe teenage girls didn't understand the appeal of a broad chest and strong forearms and . . .

Okay, so she had to get her head in the game. Ogling only led to embarrassing squeaking.

"Manly hot chocolate. Is that the difference between using jumbo marshmallows and miniature marshmallows?"

He made an odd noise, and it was only that which offered any hint to the way that could be misconstrued. Her face flamed hot and surely bright red, but no matter the embarrassment a giggle escaped her mouth.

Ask him if he's a jumbo or a mini man himself, some unknown voice in her head whispered, but the thought only made her giggle more and turn what was surely an even brighter shade of red.

"I'm going to go change," she squeaked, holding the towel somewhat over her face as she grabbed the clothes and scurried down the hall. She got to the door that she hoped she was remembering correctly as the bathroom door. She darted a look over her shoulder and

Liam was standing there with the lantern in his hands, illuminating everything around him.

Watching her. Some expression on his face she still couldn't read. Something that reminded her a little bit of years spent watching him work in her family's restaurant. Stiff, blank, maybe a little aloof.

But when his gaze met hers, she didn't think those blue eyes were any of those words. No, there was something warm, something . . . magnetic in his gaze.

Hot. He didn't break it either. They stood on opposite ends of the hall, staring at each other. Kayla's heart hammered hard against her rib cage, her pulse a noticeable thud in her throat. What would happen if she forgot about the change of clothes and just walked back down the hall. To him. What if she did all the things this more honest version of herself wanted to do?

"I'll make that hot chocolate," he said gruffly, and disappeared into the kitchen, leaving her in an eerie dark.

She let out a long breath and stepped into the bathroom, closing the door behind her. As she peeled off her sopping wet clothes in the dark, she tried to find the courage within herself to *do* something for once.

Liam didn't know what the fuck his problem was. One minute things felt very close to easy. Friendly and joking. He relaxed around her in ways it usually took him months to relax around a person.

At least when he wasn't looking at her. *Relaxed* wasn't quite what he'd felt watching her stand in the rain, her clothes plastered to the subtle curves of her body. *Easy* was not the reaction his body had felt as she'd held eye contact with him down the hallway, her cheeks faintly flushed as though . . .

He closed his eyes and took a deep breath in and a deep breath out. Yes, he was attracted to her, and maybe she was even attracted to him, but he'd played this game enough in high school to know he didn't want any part of it.

It seemed as though he and Aiden were always interested in the same women when they were in the same social circles. Liam wasn't stupid. He knew where any contest ended when it came between him and his brother.

Plenty of women liked the dependable guy well enough, but when the charming, *exciting* guy came along, it was hard not to want to be part of all that dazzle. Liam couldn't blame them. Aiden was like the sun, all bright and warm and engaging. People flocked to him.

Liam didn't want to be that guy. He didn't want to compete with Aiden, and he'd promised himself a long time ago to stop trying to be something he wasn't. He would always be dependable, responsible Liam Patrick, not just because he had to be, but because that's who he wanted to be.

How Kayla Gallagher wanted to make him forget that promise to himself was beyond his ability to reason through.

He pushed it all away. Maybe there'd been a moment. Maybe there hadn't. It didn't matter because he wasn't playing a game. He was a person. She was a person. They liked each other's company and she had the oddest interest in his wood . . .

Woodworking. Wood*working*.

He shook his head to try and get his brain to clatter into functioning in its usual, reasonable by-the-book way. He lit candles and pulled out the little backpacking stove he'd never actually used because he was always too busy to actually *go* backpacking.

He went to the sink and filled the little camping pot with water. It would be something of a process without electricity, but it was better than letting his thoughts dwell too much on wet Kayla.

"You don't make it with milk?"

He turned to face her in the entrance of his kitchen. She wore one of his T-shirts, just a plain navy blue that seemed to make her skin glow. Or maybe that was the candlelight. She had some of his sweatpants on, clearly tied as tight as possible and still a little baggy on her and definitely too long.

He could spend eternity watching her in his clothes.

"Uh, no, princess. When you're watching your pennies, you make hot chocolate with water." He walked over to the little backpacking stove he'd set on his counter and tried to look like he knew what he was doing.

"I paid you ten dollars for that bear," she said, moving next to him in the kitchen. "You could buy a gallon of milk or two. But watery cocoa is fine, as long as there are plenty of marshmallows. And if you tell me I can drink it without marshmallows, I'm going to have to call you out."

"Call me out?" he replied, his lips curving in spite of himself. She said the strangest things sometimes.

"Like a duel," she replied, matter-of-factly. The corners of her generous mouth quirked, though she clearly fought valiantly for a serious expression.

"And how does one duel in the twenty-first century?" Liam asked, stirring chocolate mix into one mug and then the next.

"Hm." She tapped a finger to her chin as though considering. "Cage fighting?"

He barked out a laugh. "I am fresh out of cages."

"You better have marshmallows then."

It was his turn to fight for a serious expression when all his mouth wanted to do was grin at her.

Oh, that's not all your mouth wants to do where she's concerned. He turned to the pantry, as much to keep his mind off his dick as to get the bag of marshmallows he hoped he had somewhere.

He rummaged around until he found a half-eaten bag in the back. He gave them a test squeeze, happy to find them not stale, then turned back to her.

He was never quite ready for that punch, no matter how many times in the past few days he'd turned to find her in his house, in his space. It was a jolt every time. A little zap of electric current, like touching an exposed wire.

"Marshmallows," he managed, lamely holding out the bag.

She pulled her bottom lip through her teeth, slowly and very, *very* distractingly, and then on a deep breath she moved toward him.

She took the bag and then set it down on the counter. She took a deep breath, odd and out of place, as though she had to build up the courage to drink some hot chocolate, which didn't make any sense—

Then she stepped closer. Close enough that their toes were practically touching, close enough that she had to tilt back her head to meet his gaze. Close enough that if he *didn't* meet her gaze he could see the faint points of her nipples through the thin fabric of his T-shirt that she wore.

She stood there, close, her breathing a little shallow and her hands moving out as though to touch him, then falling abruptly to her sides, then inching closer again.

He was rendered speechless and possibly motionless for a few seconds. She was standing practically pressed against him, apparently nervous and uncertain and what else could she be possibly thinking but . . .

It baffled him that she'd have any reason to be nervous about making a move on him. Didn't she know he'd fall at her feet a million times over?

If she didn't, then he supposed it was his job to assure her of it. He was a fixer after all.

He cupped her cheek, letting his fingertips explore the cool, soft texture of her skin. He stepped closer, widening his stance so that she fit against him, her legs between his, her chest against his.

His body thrummed with that current, that zip of life and power and spark. He lowered his mouth, slowly, giving her all the chances in the world to—not retreat exactly. His hold on her face wasn't going anywhere, but she had the chance to say something, to ward him off.

She didn't use that chance. His mouth touched hers, something unknown shuddering through him. Something unfamiliar flickering into life. A warmth, a centering as though he'd been waiting for just this. Always.

Which didn't make any sense, but what did make sense was the way her body fit against his, the way her arms tentatively and then tightly wound around his neck. The way her mouth opened under his, a wet hot invitation to invade.

Which was not an invitation he'd decline in any universe. He swept his tongue over her lips and into her mouth, drowning in a flavor he'd never even let himself guess at.

Kayla Gallagher tasted like summer-sun-soaked berries. Sweet and warm and a bright, a delectable contrast to every damn dreary thing in his life.

She made some sound, a moan or sigh, and it made the hand on her cheek not nearly enough. He stroked one palm down the soft, elegant curve of her neck, let his other hand tangle in the wet red waves of hair—a shining beacon on a woman who'd always seemed so bent on hiding.

Until recently, anyway. She'd been the one to invite herself here, to step forward, and he may have been the one to kiss her, but it never would have happened if not for her first move.

It should feel dreamlike, but instead her body was a warm, delicious reality against him. He smoothed his palm down her spine and she arched into him, and there was no way she could miss the hard ridge of his erection against her midsection.

Would he feel the same response from her? If he tugged off his own sweatpants from her body and slid his hands between her legs, would she be as wet for him as he was hard for her from just a kiss?

His hands itched to do just that, to slide over her ass to the front of her pants and undo the flimsy knot that kept him from knowing.

She licked into his mouth, pressing more firmly against him, her fingers rifling through his hair, and it took every ounce of reason and restraint to keep his hands above her clothes.

Not everyone leaped ahead like he did. He'd been made aware of that a few more times than he cared to remember. Women always seemed to find him a little *too* something—his high school girlfriend had found the fact he had hair on his chest "problematic." His last girlfriend had decided after a few months that he was just too "traditionally masculine."

And everything he wanted to do with Kayla was very, very traditionally masculine. He wanted his cock inside of her and his mouth all over her skin. He wanted to know what every inch of her tasted like, and he wanted to hear her scream his name.

"Liam." It was a whisper, but it was damn good enough.

Her head had fallen back and her eyes fluttered open, that dark blue meeting his gaze with a dazed kind of satisfaction, but it was the way her mouth curved into something very close to a self-satisfied smirk that just about did him in.

He splayed his hands on her lower back, sliding them over the curve of her ass, pulling her closer, settling the length of his erection between her legs and giving a little thrust.

Her head fell back even farther and she sighed, fingers digging into the back of his neck. She was stunning, the length of her pale neck exposed and glowing in the light of the candles and the camping lantern, her hair waving out of the braid she'd haphazardly put it in as it dried from the rain. Her eyes were half closed, though she watched him carefully.

He wanted to scrape his teeth across her neck. He wanted to grip his hands into her red shimmering hair. He wanted to do a million things that would probably be deemed *too much*.

So he settled himself on the least *too much* course of action he could think of. He held her gaze as he moved his hands to the front of her pants and found the tie. He tugged the string loose. She didn't move, didn't break eye contact, just looked at him, her arms still around his neck as the fabric fell to the ground.

She made another one of those noises, something that almost reminded him of a cat purring, as she trailed her fingertips down his chest and abdomen. She tugged at the hem of his shirt, lifting it as far as she could manage before he had to help her get it over his head.

It fell to the floor with her sweatpants. She inhaled sharply and for a second of intense disappointment, he was certain this was the moment where she decided it—he—was that little bit too much.

Instead, she reached out and put a palm to his chest, her fingers splaying across the hair there, then following the trail down to the waistband of his shorts. She paused, her eyebrows knitting together as if contemplating something of grave importance.

He wanted to touch her, feel the rough of his hands against the soft, creamy skin of her thighs, the hot wet center of her, but he willed himself to give her a second to figure out whatever problem she was trying to solve.

On another one of those courage-rallying deep breaths, she leaned forward and pressed a kiss to the center of his chest, and then higher, then where his beard met neck, and then his mouth, just a gentle brush of her berry-flavored lips, even as her fingertips moved softly across where his shorts hung on his hips.

She looked up at him through thick, burnished-gold lashes. "I don't suppose you have any condoms?" she asked, her fingers dipping under the waistband of his shorts, teasingly far away from where he wanted them.

"Um, no." Though he'd run out and get some first thing in the morning without hesitation. "But we do have hands and mouths," he offered, a little too drunk on her proximity, on her taste, on how fucking gorgeous she was to care about anything being *too much*.

Her entire hand slid under his shorts and boxers, her cool, slim fingers wrapping around his throbbing cock. "I suppose that'll do," she returned with mock seriousness, before flashing him a grin.

Chapter Eight

Kayla had a man's penis in her hand. Not just any man's penis, *Liam Patrick's* penis. And not because they'd been going out for a certain amount of dates or months. Just because she'd wanted to.

He was hot and hard in her palm and when she stroked, that electric blue of his eyes never once wavered from hers. The intensity there, the heat, made her breath back up in her lungs, but it didn't make her stop.

Because she had been *changed* over the course of her too-long break from Gallagher's and that old Kayla she didn't want to recognize was gone. She had been changed in Liam's workshop, altered in the rain.

She was blooming, and being brave, and taking something she wanted. She was throwing herself into the fire of confusion and emotion and something complicated instead of running away from all those things.

She stroked him again, watching the way his eyes seemed to turn into blue crystal, prisms of light, and she wanted that grim certainty he had lurking there, as though he knew everything about his place in the world.

But more, so much more, she wanted *him*. That kiss. His touch. Her body already *yearned* for something she'd only just experienced, and damned if she'd be too afraid to get it.

"Touch me," she forced herself to say, and no matter that her words were a shaky, nervy whisper, or that her whole body recoiled at the thought of embarrassing herself, she'd *said* it.

And he did.

His mouth crushed to hers, hot and demanding, his arms around her in a tight band, trapping her arm exactly where it was—between them, fingers curled around his erection incapable of moving to stroke, but she forgot all about that as he kissed her. A kiss made of lips and tongue and teeth, a wildness she'd never experienced in herself, in someone else. There was no timidity, no question, and most of all no attempt to maneuver things any which way.

He was simply kissing her as if she was the air he needed to breathe, and she held on to him like floating debris in a stormy ocean. She felt unmoored and free, full of electricity and something . . . unnameable.

Usually no matter how long she'd been with someone, physical intimacy was nerve-wracking. She never knew quite what a guy expected of her, what he might want from her, it always felt as if there was some special secret she'd never been privy to, and she'd definitely never known how to ask for the answers.

But with Liam she didn't feel nerves or questions. Not in this moment with his mouth desperate on hers and his arms banded around her.

His tight grip loosened, his hands sliding down her back and then she felt her shirt lifting. Since her underwear and bra had been soaked through, she'd discarded them with her other clothes. Which meant with the sweatpants gone and the shirt being lifted off her head, she was completely naked. In Liam's kitchen. Just naked.

In some dim part of her brain she thought she should feel silly or embarrassed maybe, but he looked at her as no man had ever looked at her. As though she were some work of art, some goddess worthy of worship.

He muttered a curse, but his hands were immeasurably gentle as he cupped her face and then slid down her neck. Big and warm, that and the cool of the room causing her skin to goose bump, her nipples to pull into tight points.

But Liam kept touching her, and it warmed away any chill in the room. His rough hands molded over her body like he was a sculptor forming her into something else entirely, or she was sculpting herself, or this moment was, because she didn't feel like herself. She felt better than she ever had.

His hands palmed her breasts and his mouth found her neck, an openmouthed kiss before his teeth scraped gently down the slope to her shoulder.

She moaned and it sounded overloud to her ears, but she hardly cared as his thumbs brushed her nipples, as he pulled her body to his and she could feel the hard length of his cock through his shorts pressing against her.

It really was a shame they didn't have condoms. She wanted to know what it would be like to be filled and stretched by him. Would it have the same magic this moment seemed to have, or would it be the same as every other mildly entertaining sexual encounter she'd experienced?

Liam's hands smoothed down her sides and to her hips, holding her there as he pressed himself against her, his mouth moving from her neck to the top of her breasts.

She felt like she was shuddering apart, and it was getting harder to breathe evenly. Her heart beat hard, as if she'd run a race, and then his tongue touched her nipple. She swallowed to keep from squeaking, blinking down at his dark head over her chest. She seemed to pulse in time with the flicks of his tongue.

But when he sucked her nipple deep into his mouth, the pulse was a sharp, needy pang that made her knees buckle.

He laughed against her breast—actually *laughed*—and she wanted to laugh too. Instead, she held on to his shoulders and righted herself, but he didn't continue. Instead, he straightened, but as he did he linked his hands under her ass and lifted. She let out a half gasp, half laugh and looked down to see his eyes sparkling with what was sure to prove to be a very *dirty* mischief.

"Grab the lantern," he ordered.

She leaned forward to grab the handle of the lantern that was on the counter behind him, one hand still clutched on his shoulder. Not that he seemed to have any problem carrying her.

His lips brushed against her collarbone as he walked, as though she weighed next to nothing, out of the kitchen and down the hall. His bristled cheek brushed against her dampened, needy nipple—whether out of accident or design—and she jolted at the amazing pop of pleasure.

"Steady," he murmured, nudging the door to his bedroom open with his elbow.

Steady? She was vibrating with a million things, and most of them were good things. But she couldn't manage steady or easy or even breathing that wasn't heavy.

Liam lowered her onto the bed, taking the lantern from her grasp and placing it on to a nightstand next to the bed. Then he was over her, so tall and broad and . . .

She sighed dreamily. She loved that she could tell just from looking at the curve of his arms as he held himself above her that he was strong enough to carry her around. She already loved the way the whiskers of his beard scratched against her skin. And she loved that he could smile *and* look at her like he wanted to devour her at the same time.

"If you don't like anything, tell me to stop," he said, his eyes diamond blue on hers, his voice threaded with graveled seriousness.

She blinked at him and she supposed for some people that would be obvious, but to her it was like a revelation. She could and *should* speak up when she didn't like something, when she wanted something else.

That had never truly occurred to her before, not in that serious, straightforward way. She'd always figured with sex or anything leading up to sex you were supposed to say what the other person wanted to hear, do what the other person expected of you.

He watched her expectantly, waiting for her response. Was there a response to that that wasn't an enthusiastic, *Yes, sir*. "O-okay," she managed to say

This was all astonishing. Liam Patrick's mouth had been on her breasts. He'd touched her everywhere except where she pulsed, needy and desperate for him. Liam *Patrick*.

He wasn't that gruff, disapproving figure she'd made up in her mind. Liam was none of the things she'd assumed of him or attributed to him. He was warm and he was kind. He called himself a fixer, but what he really did was *help* people.

Because he could, and because he felt like he should.

He carved lovespoons and read up on symbols. He went to mass because his grandmother wanted him to. And he'd kissed her like she wasn't some timid, fragile thing.

She rubbed her fingertips over his bearded jaw, in awe of so many things about Liam.

"What do you want, Kayla?" he murmured, brushing a kiss against her mouth, and then her shoulder. He kept one hand pressed to the mattress by her waist, keeping his weight off of her, but his other hand drew patterns down her arm, across her stomach.

Still, agonizingly still, he hadn't touched her where she most wanted him. What did she want? She took a deep breath, steeling herself to ask for something. She'd learned to refuse things she didn't want, and that had been hard once, but asking for what she *did* was untested. New.

Fucking terrifying.

Be brave. Be brave.

"Touch my . . ." She couldn't quite make her mouth form the word. Surely he knew what she was getting at. That was close enough, right?

But he raised an eyebrow, as if daring her, and *damn it*, she was brave. She could say dirty words. She could demand things she wanted. "Touch my pussy, Liam."

His mouth curved into a grin she'd never seen on him. Nearly wolfish and self-satisfied. Unbearably handsome. "Have you never said that word before?"

She laughed nervously. "Uh, no. At least not during sex, or almost sex, or yes, probably ever."

"My daring Kayla," he murmured, dropping his mouth to hers, even as his hand slid down her abdomen, and then her thigh, pushing her legs open.

Daring. His. She liked the idea of both of those.

And then he stroked, one long, blunt finger tracing her. She made a strangled sound, fidgeting restlessly underneath him. Each stroke was slow, delicious torture. Too light, too easy. She needed more, so much more.

"Liam."

"Hmm?"

She huffed out an irritated breath. Usually these things went fairly quickly and she didn't have to do any talking, but usually they didn't feel like this. Like she was nothing but fissuring light, pleasure and desperation, and a sharp clawing feeling in her chest that things would not be okay until Liam was on top of her, inside of her.

"More," she said, and her voice wasn't the least bit stuttering or whispered this time. She demanded it, loud and sure. "More, please."

And though she'd told him, he was still far too slow about it. His finger sliding only incrementally deeper with each stroke, but it was like drowning in ecstasy, a wonderful pleasure, a wonderful need, but she needed more of it. She needed so much more of it.

His mouth trailed down her chest, her stomach, and it took her far too long to realize what he was doing. It didn't fully come together in her head until he slid off the bed and pulled her easily until her ass was at the edge.

Her chest clenched, a hard fist of nerves. No one had ever . . . She wasn't even really sure she'd ever wanted someone to. It seemed so . . .

"I didn't mean that you had to . . ." But his tongue touched her, one long, slow, delicious slide of friction, deeper and more insistent than his finger had been. His dark hair between her legs, his big, scarred hands on her thighs.

"Did you want me to stop?" he asked, his gaze meeting hers over the length of her body. His eyes fierce and sharp, and everything about the moment a little bit scary and yet she was brave and daring and that had felt so *very* good.

"No," she whispered.

She thought maybe she caught the quirk of his mouth before it returned to her pussy—a word she'd said *aloud*—and then as his tongue entered her, she forgot everything. She'd kind of wanted to watch, but the pleasure was too much, her eyes squeezed shut. Her body moved compulsively against his mouth.

She could feel his beard against her inner thighs, and somehow he was licking at her, into her, and using his fingers. When his tongue flicked across her clit, her gasp was loud and echoing.

She had to fist her hands in the sheets to keep from bucking off the bed, to keep from pressing herself against him, and still Liam licked and sucked and seemed determined to make her gasp again and again and again.

She was hot, too hot, and everything inside of her was coiled too tight. She realized belatedly she was chanting his name, and as he slid two fingers inside of her, his tongue pressing against her clit, she shuddered apart into a blistering, sparkling orgasm. Wave after wave, moving through her like nothing else—no one else—ever had.

She realized she'd been bucking against his mouth as much as his arms around her legs had allowed, but once she stilled he slid his arms from around her legs. He kissed her inner thigh, and then the other, then her belly button, slowly crawling back over her.

The grin on his face was impossible not to return. She felt dazed and dazzled, and he seemed so contained, so perfectly happy to have given her something.

So she reached out, quickly shoving her hands under his shorts and grabbing the hot, hard length of him. She held him in one hand as she tugged down his shorts and boxers with the other, and then she got to her knees.

He'd broken her apart with only his mouth and hands, and now it was her turn to do the same to him.

Liam was pretty sure he'd lost his mind somewhere along the way. Maybe he'd been electrocuted in his workshop and this was a very elaborate dream.

But he kneeled next to Kayla on his bed, and her hands felt very real as they smoothed up and down his thighs.

Her tongue felt more than real as it slowly licked up the length of his dick. At the very tip, she flicked a gaze up at him, swirling her tongue around.

He groaned low and guttural and though some rational part of his brain told him not to, he settled his hands around her scalp, threading his fingers through her hair, urging her mouth to take him inside.

She didn't hesitate, didn't fight the slight pressure of his palms. She just opened and drew him in, a slow, slick slide. It was as if his entire existence was centered there, her pretty pink lips around his thick shaft.

Sucking him in, drawing him out, her hands balanced on his thighs, her red hair a riot of flame around her pale, freckled face. The beautiful pink of her nipples drawn to a point and moving in time with her gentle bobbing.

He tried to think beyond the need to curl his fingers in her hair, tug her closer, make her take him deeper, but the more she moved her mouth up and down his cock, the more thinking was impossible.

She didn't even jerk away or look at him alarmed as his fingers curled tighter into her hair. If anything, she simply sighed against him and took him deeper into her mouth.

"You like it?" he asked, his voice rough at best, but he wasn't sure he could trust his own eyes. He needed some kind of confirmation, some kind of . . .

She pulled back, though her lips didn't quite leave the head. "Yes," she breathed, and he jerked at the bolt of ecstasy that was her breath against his wet cock. "Do you?" she whispered, causing another jerk and his hands to tighten in her hair even more.

"Yeah, I like your pretty mouth on my cock." He shouldn't say things like that. He knew he shouldn't. But she moaned against him as though she liked it, taking him deep in the wet heat of her mouth.

His eyes fluttered closed, but he fought it, wanting to watch her face, her pale, slim fingers splayed over his hips. The way her lips stretched around him, drawing him in and out. Kayla. This beautiful, sweet, once-timid woman. The taste of her pussy on his tongue, her blue eyes looking up at him from her bent-over position.

He could feel himself tightening, the crushing blow of climax just a few more swirls of her tongue away.

"Kayla." He tried to pull her back and away, but she only sucked him deeper, her nails faintly digging into his thighs. So he surrendered to it, the orgasm, holding her there as it roared through him. His body pulsed, his vision suffused with some sparkling light and Kayla's dark blue eyes watching him through the whole thing.

Slowly, she pulled off of him, and he supposed he should let go of her hair so she could pull completely away, but he didn't want to let her go. Even limp and satisfied he wanted her right here.

He tugged her head up, bending his own down, brushing his mouth across her swollen one. Her mouth curved, as self-satisfied as he'd ever seen a person, and it made him smile in return.

"You know, if this wasn't what you were trying to start back in the kitchen, I'm going to be a little embarrassed," he managed to say as he finally forced himself to unclench his fingers from her silky hair.

"Only a little?" she asked, rubbing a palm against his jaw, still so damn satisfied he had no doubt she was teasing.

"You seemed to enjoy it all right even if it's not what you intended."

She laughed, the sound lazy and husky as she stretched out and laid back on the bed. "Mm. I'm pretty sure that's what I intended."

He looked down at her and wondered if he'd ever forget the image of Kayla Gallagher naked in his bed. Maybe he should take it all at face value, but he'd been burned a few times in that department.

Carefully, he pulled up his boxers and shorts. He lay beside her, mirroring her sprawled position. He stared at the ceiling, hoping the words didn't come out stupid. "So that wasn't uh . . . too much?"

"I feel very much like *just right* Goldilocks right now." She stretched her arms out, walking two fingers across his chest and back until he looked at her. She grinned. "Definitely not too much."

"Good," he managed lamely. Her riot of red hair was tangled across his pillow, her skin a slight pink where his mouth or hands or beard had been.

She yawned, curling toward him on her side, her hand resting lightly on his chest. Her eyes were half closed, but the smug little smile hadn't left her face.

Just right, yes she was.

"I could run out and get some condoms," he murmured sleepily, everything about getting off Kayla's warm body making him sluggish. But sex seemed like a good idea, in a minute or two, once the use of his muscles returned.

Kayla's eyes had completely closed though. "Mm," was her only reply, her breathing slow and even.

He should probably set his alarm. He had early appointments in the morning, but all he managed was to pull the discarded bedspread up and over the both of them and fall asleep.

Chapter Nine

"Shit, shit, shit."

Kayla was jerked out of sleep by that repeated word and the bed she was in moving as though she were in an earthquake.

She blinked her eyes open, realizing for the second time in a week she was in Liam's bed.

Heat suffused her cheeks this time though because she was quite sure of all the things she'd done with Liam last night. There was no fuzzy memory or wondering what might have happened.

She remembered it all in great detail.

"Shit," he was muttering over and over, pawing around in drawers, pulling on a pair of jeans and then a T-shirt.

"What's wrong?"

He didn't spare her a glance. "I'm supposed to meet my dad at seven to go over some business stuff before our first appointment of the day."

Kayla glanced at the old digital clock on his nightstand. Well, shit was right. It was already seven.

"Is there anything I can do? Do you need me to—"

"You're fine," he said, plopping down on the bed and pulling on socks hurriedly. "Take your time, feel free to eat anything in the kitchen, and I'll leave you my key so you can lock up."

"But how will you get back in?"

"I'll stop by your place on my way home from work." He popped off the bed again, grabbing his phone and shoving it into his pocket.

"Oh, okay," Kayla managed, still drowsy with sleep and not quite putting everything he said together. Except he was leaving, which was not exactly how she'd planned to spend the morning.

"Sorry." He gave her a hurried kiss and almost missed her mouth completely, just hitting the corner. "I'm never late." And with that, he strode into the bathroom.

His words made her smile. No, Liam wasn't the type of man who would be late. She never would have listed *punctual* as an attribute she needed in a man, but the thing about Liam never being late was that it spoke not just to his deep sense of responsibility, but to the fact he was a man you could trust.

The kind of man who'd put a woman, if not first, at least on equal ground. He cared that other people were okay, and if they weren't, he wanted to help. That was quite the amazing thing.

She had the terrible tendency of dating guys who treated her as more of an afterthought. Someone to pursue, but ultimately be bored with the moment the catch had been made.

Come to think of it, that's probably what had happened with Aiden. He'd been interested until she'd so enthusiastically said yes to him asking her out.

Kayla bit her lip as she pulled the blankets up to her chin. Truth be told, she hadn't thought about Aiden in days. Had she put Liam in an awkward position by ending up falling for him instead?

She rolled her eyes at herself. Yes, because Aiden had been *so* interested. Interested enough to miss their date, send his brother, and spend the next few days not contacting her in any way.

Yeah, Aiden was fine.

Liam came out of the bathroom, keys in hand. He was twisting what she presumed to be his house key off a ring. "My last appointment should be over around five. Will you be home?"

"I should be."

He placed the key on the nightstand. "I'll text first, but I'll swing by and pick it up. Sound good?"

Kayla nodded. He shoved his keys into his pockets, giving her only the most cursory glance.

"I'll see you later then," he muttered, and was walking quickly out the bedroom door before he'd finished the sentence.

Kayla watched him go. She should get up and get dressed and get out of his house. She had résumés to send out, job listings to scour. She had things to do. But before she could put her mind to any of them, Liam reappeared.

"Fuck it," he said emphatically, and for the first time this morning his eyes were on her. Fierce and hot, like she was something he had to possess. The shiver that went through her had nothing to do with fear and everything to do with excitement, and then she was crushed against him, his mouth hot and wild on hers, his tongue delving into her mouth with no preamble.

She wound her arms around his neck and he all but pulled her off the bed with simply the strength of his arms around her.

No one, ever, had kissed her like she was something both precious and *necessary*. No one, ever, had made her feel this heart-pumping desire mixed with some chest-constricting warmth. But Liam made her feel both things, and so many more unnameable reactions.

He pulled his mouth away, though his arms remained around her, keeping her pulled slightly above being prone on the bed. He was breathing heavily, a bit of a dazed expression on his face.

She had dazed him. *Her*. It was that power from last night. It was a giddy rightness. All things she'd never had. Never known she'd *wanted*. But oh, *oh*, she wanted him and all he could do to her.

His crystal-blue eyes ablaze with something Kayla felt like she understood on some cellular level even though she couldn't put it into words. She just knew it was . . . more. So much more than she was used to.

And she liked it.

"Stop and get condoms before you come over tonight," she managed to say, though she was panting as if she'd run a mile.

His mouth curved, sharp and all the more lethal because he employed it so infrequently. "I might forget my own name, but I will not forget the condoms."

"Now, go," she urged, smiling at him. "I hear you're never late."

The smile he wore now was softer, the quirk of one side. Responsible, kind Liam as opposed to feral, lustful Liam. So many facets to this man she never would have guessed at.

"I'll see you soon," he replied, giving her one quick kiss before letting her go completely. He stepped out of the room, glancing back once and offering a wave.

She knew she was probably letting her heart lead and gallop ahead when it would be more sensible and responsible to keep her feelings in check, to wait and see how things went. She should be careful if only to avoid getting hurt.

But she was always careful. Always waiting for someone else to make the first move or show her the next step, and the thing was, it had never once stopped her from getting hurt. Being the timid, *fragile* doormat didn't keep you from getting stepped on or broken. It just kept other people from having to see they'd done it.

No more. Improved . . . Well, "Improving Kayla" was not going to be cautious. She was going to embrace this new hand she'd been dealt.

And if Liam wasn't on the same page, well, she'd survive. She'd at the very least get some sex out of the deal—and if actual sex was anything like last night, it would well be worth a little heartache.

"You got a girl."

Liam jerked at Dad's accusation as he bandaged up the scrape across his knuckles. He didn't bother to look up and into what would be Dad's too-shrewd gaze. He focused on getting a bandage over the cut.

"Girl?"

"Girl. Woman. Whatever. You're never this distracted, son. Hell, you had better focus when you had mono."

Liam shot Dad a wry glance. "Exaggerate much?" Except maybe today it wasn't that big of an exaggeration. He'd thought about Kayla all day. Too much. Far too much. He was a guy who liked sex. What guy didn't? Sometimes he'd wondered if it was a bit much, all in all, but it had never been this bad, this all-encompassing need.

But this whole distraction thing wasn't solely about sex or the almost having of it. It had more to do with the woman herself.

"Well, since you aren't sick, best as I can tell, it's got to be a woman."

"Maybe it is." Liam finished with his bandage and then went to his toolbox to put away his tools. It was already almost five o'clock and he'd put in a full day with Dad. He still needed to stop somewhere and buy condoms, actually use said condoms with Kayla, and, if he had an ounce of sense left in his head, he'd go home and do some work in his shop for the market on Wednesday.

"Going to tell me about her?"

Liam shrugged. He supposed he could tell Dad that it was Kayla Gallagher, but if he told Dad, Dad would tell Mom, who would mention it to Aiden, and as of yet Liam hadn't had any luck getting ahold of Aiden to tell him that his little plan of getting Kayla was over.

She was Liam's now.

Some people would probably consider that a pretty archaic way of thinking, and those people could go fuck themselves.

He locked his toolbox and nodded to Dad as they headed out of the Coreli's house where they'd managed to fiddle with their ancient dishwasher enough to get it working again.

"Not getting any younger," Dad commented as he pulled open the truck bed so Liam could shove the toolbox into its spot.

Liam gave his father a doleful look as he fastened the box to the truck bed. "Neither are you, and yet you won't retire."

Dad grunted and let the subject drop as Liam had known he would. Dad didn't want to discuss retirement, and Liam wasn't sure he wanted to discuss Kayla quite yet, so that worked out all in all.

They both climbed into the company truck and Liam watched out the window as Dad drove them back home. Liam glanced at Dad, then shifted as casually as he could to pull his phone out of his pocket.

"I don't suppose you're calling your mother to let her know we're on the way?" Dad asked, so innocently Liam snorted.

"No." He warred with himself for a second, then went ahead and typed a text to Kayla, Dad's smugness be damned.

Dad pulled the truck up the driveway of Mom and Dad's house and they both got out. Dad gestured toward the door.

"Don't suppose you'd want to come in and have dinner with me and your mom?"

"I, uh, have plans."

"Of course you do," Dad replied with a genuine smile, but it faded almost as quickly as it had bloomed. "Don't suppose you know anything about where your brother's disappeared to?"

Liam sighed and shook his head. "No."

Dad sighed too and Liam noted how similarly it sounded to his. Was he already turning into his father? Did that bother him? Liam wasn't sure. He loved and respected his father more than any other man in his life, and he . . . Well, he had certain flimsy ideas of what a future might look like *some* day, and it looked a heck of a lot like what Dad had built.

"Your mother's worried," Dad said, taking his hat off his head and mashing it between his hands. Mom never let him wear it in the house.

"Should *we* be?" Liam asked, feeling a little prick of guilt over the fact he hadn't concerned himself with Aiden's disappearance.

Dad shook his head as he stared at the house, as though he could see Mom worried inside of it. "Doubt it. He told your mother he'd be gone a few weeks 'tying up some loose ends,' but she thought he was acting squirrelly."

"Isn't he always?" Liam muttered before he could stop himself.

"That's what I said." Dad smiled, but the serious look in his eye gave Liam pause.

"Everything okay?" Liam asked, as casually as he could. Though he knew his dad could be serious when it came to business and what not, his usual outward demeanor was one of jovial good fun. But in the years since his heart attack, serious moments seemed to creep up, and they never failed to make Liam uncomfortable.

"I hope you know how much your mother and I appreciate you."

Liam could only stare, wide eyed and frozen at his father's uncharacteristic show of gratitude.

"I . . . Sure. Sure, I do," Liam said, though considering the shock the statement had produced in him, maybe he hadn't quite. Or maybe it was nice to hear.

"You're the glue, Liam. Always have been. Glue can get overlooked sometimes, because it's not as flashy as the things it's holding together, but it's the most important thing. I know even as adults Aiden gets most of the attention, but that doesn't mean we don't appreciate the fact that you've stuck it out and worked hard for this family."

"You sure everything's okay?" Liam asked, because he couldn't help but think this little speech spoke to a larger problem. It might be genuine, but it wasn't ordinary.

Dad quirked a smile as he sighed. "Dinah Gallagher mentioned you have a table at that farmers' market they've started over there."

Liam had no words for that. He'd never planned on telling his parents about the farmers' market, and never considered they might find out.

"If you aren't happy . . . I don't want to be the reason—"

"It's a hobby, Dad. Honestly." He stepped toward his father, not knowing how to put into words the complexity of what he felt. Patrick's was something like his soul, the woodworking something like his heart, and that was shit he could not say to his father. "Patrick & Son means the world to me. The farmers' market . . . It's just a thing to do."

Dad stared at him, something like pain etched on his face. Pain and age, and Liam hated seeing it there. Hated that insidious knowledge that his parents were aging, that *he* was aging, that no matter what he fixed or built, he'd never be able to make all this stay the same.

"Dad, I need you to believe that, because it is the God's honest truth. Whether you want me to be part of Patrick's or not, it's mine."

Dad gave a sharp nod and something of a forced smile. "Good. Good. Go see that woman of yours, then, and know we'd like to meet her whenever that's something you want to do."

"Uh. Sure." It filled him with some feeling he couldn't identify, the idea of bringing Kayla to dinner with his family. Not even because there could be weirdness with Aiden, but because he had no doubt she'd charm his parents within seconds, and she'd be charmed in return.

Yeah, he didn't know what that gut twist was at all. "See you tomorrow, Dad."

Dad waved and headed for the door and Liam stood in his parents' driveway trying to breathe through the uncomfortable feeling that something was wrong.

But what was there to do about it? The problem with Dad was Liam couldn't bulldoze him into answers. The more Liam insisted he needed to explain what was wrong, the more Dad would clam up. All Liam could do was step back and wait.

Fuck, he hated that.

He shoved a hand through his hair and turned to his truck parked on the street. Well, he had something to distract him, didn't he? He glanced at his phone. Kayla hadn't texted him back, but he still had to find a drugstore and buy some condoms, and then get to her place. It'd take long enough.

So he focused on that, pushing everything his dad had said as far out of his mind as he could. There was nothing to do, no way to fix, not until Dad allowed it. And Liam was shit with things he couldn't fix so . . .

Well, shit and damn was about all there was to it. He drove to the drugstore and bought the condoms before driving to Kayla's apartment complex that didn't fit her at all. He was distracted and vaguely irritated. With himself. With Dad. He shoved his phone into his glove compartment because hell if he was going to let work interrupt this.

He was halfway up her staircase before he realized she'd never texted him back. Luckily he remembered the apartment number she'd given him. He paused briefly, but in the end he figured he might as well knock and see if she was home and if not he'd go retrieve his phone.

When the door swung open to reveal Kayla, fresh faced with her red hair all pulled back into a sloppy ponytail, her mouth curving at the sight of him, every tense, irritable thing inside of him uncoiled.

"Liam. I just called—"

Maybe he should have let her finish, but he couldn't seem to stop himself. He swooped down and captured her mouth with his, wrapping his arms around her and walking her into the apartment.

She sighed into his mouth, winding her arms around his neck, kissing him back almost as desperately as he'd kissed her. He kicked the door behind him closed and dropped the plastic bag of condoms on the floor, because if he had his way they'd be on the ground soon enough.

"Oh." She pulled her mouth from his. "Wait."

Wait? For what? Hell, he was dying. He kissed down her neck, his hands sliding under her shirt and up the elegant curve of her back.

She laughed, giving him the lightest, most ineffective push ever. "Liam. Really."

"Really what?" he asked before sliding his fingers under the waistband of her pants so he could cup the hot, soft skin of her ass.

She sighed, relaxing for a second before she gave him another half-hearted push. "No. Really. You have to stop!"

So he did, though it all but killed him. He was aching, hard, and desperate for her, and she was telling him to stop. He pulled his hands out of her pants and looked down at her pained face.

She reached up and rubbed her palm against his bearded jaw with a wistful sigh. His chest tightened hard, and he didn't know what that was either. He was tired of this "not understanding his own feelings" shit, and the only way to fix that was to talk her into bed, he was pretty sure.

"I have company coming."

Or not. "Company?"

"I forgot all about it this morning. I guess I was distracted, but—"

"Oh." He untangled himself from her, feeling like a fucking moron. Company. She had mysterious company and he'd thought . . . Well, he'd been a dipshit to think.

"It's just—" A knock interrupted whatever Kayla's explanation was going to be, and maybe that was for the best.

"I'm sorry I forgot, but . . ." She trailed off lamely, walking toward the door.

"Want me to hide or something?" Because he didn't know what else *company* might mean other than another date. He supposed it could be friends, but why would she call it *company* if it was just a group of friends?

Hell, it could be Aiden for all he knew. What an awful thought.

She cocked her head. "You don't need to hide."

She opened the door and Liam could only stare at the woman on the other side of it. Polished and pretty, he'd recognize Dinah Gallagher anywhere.

Clearly, she recognized him as well. Her eyes widened at the sight of him before returning to Kayla.

"I . . . can come back?" Dinah offered with an officious businesswoman-looking smile.

"No. No, Liam was just . . ." Kayla looked back at him, trailing off with her mouth still open.

"Leaving," he finished for her. "The sink's all fixed, Ms. Gallagher."

Kayla's eyebrows drew together as he walked past her and Dinah, but Liam just kept walking. Clearly he'd screwed everything up, so now he was fixing it.

She didn't want Dinah to think anything was going on, so it wasn't. There was no reason that should bother him. No reason his teeth should be gritted together or his stomach should still have that same sick feeling it had had when he'd imagined Aiden on the other side of that door.

It was fine. Good even.

"Liam?"

She stood at the top of the stairs he'd walked halfway down and he turned to face her, though he was tempted to just keep walking. Her face was bathed in the odd orange glow of the apartment exterior lights. She looked confused, and maybe a little hurt.

Surely he was reading into things.

She walked down so that she was only a step above him. She looked at him as if she expected him to say something, but he didn't know what she wanted from him.

Finally she leaned down and brushed a kiss across his mouth. "Tomorrow?"

And she looked genuinely worried, as though he'd reject her. Which was the craziest damn thing. Surely she didn't think that was *possible*. Not when she was so sweet and gorgeous and he was a cranky ass.

"Tomorrow," he repeated with a nod. This whole mix-up of a night didn't matter. He wouldn't let it.

Her smile was quick and beautiful and no matter that he felt a little . . . weird about her wanting to keep things from her family, he supposed it was best for both of them. God knew he had to keep it from his until he was sure Aiden had moved on from his little plan.

It was for the best really. Besides, maybe his mood would best be assuaged in his workshop rather than by having sex with Kayla.

He rolled his eyes at himself. In what fucking lifetime?

Chapter Ten

Kayla moved slowly back into her apartment. She didn't have any earthly idea what had just happened. Liam had been . . .

Well, *first* he'd been super-hot. No one had ever kissed her the minute her door was opened as if they had been *starved* for her all day.

Then, he'd lied to Dinah. Easily. As though people shouldn't know they were . . . doing whatever it was they were doing. Kayla stepped back into her apartment trying to fix a smile on to her face, and failing miserably.

"What on God's green earth is *Liam Patrick* doing in your apartment?" Dinah demanded, all but pouncing on her. "I want every detail. Especially if they're dirty."

Kayla's cheeks heated and she was probably bright red at this point, which meant lying was pointless. She'd never been any good at lying to Dinah. It was half of why she'd had to separate herself from Dinah in the grand claiming of her life.

"I don't buy the sink thing for a second, so you might as well spill," Dinah said, crossing her arms over her chest and grinning.

"Um." Kayla blew out a breath and marched into the kitchen. "I need wine for this conversation."

"Ooh. Exciting." Dinah followed her into the little postage stamp of a kitchen. "You . . . haven't done much around your place."

"No." Kayla grabbed one of the bottles of wine Dinah had set on the counter next to her corkscrew. She went to work opening the bottle without bothering to elaborate.

"Is there a safe topic here?" Dinah asked softly.

Kayla closed her eyes and sighed. Maybe there wasn't. Maybe nothing was safe or easy, and maybe she had to deal with it.

"I haven't done anything with this place because I hate it."

"Kay—"

She didn't want Dinah's sympathy, or whatever offer of help she was likely to give, so Kayla bulldozed on. "And I don't know exactly what's going on with Liam." She poured herself a very generous glass of wine before handing the bottle and an empty glass to Dinah. Maybe an hour ago she would have had a more certain answer, but the last ten minutes with Liam had made everything . . . confusing.

"But it's dirty, right? That was a dirty vibe."

Kayla laughed. No matter how confused she felt about it, Dinah had a way of zeroing in on the easy thing. Always giving Kayla the simple way out. Was that what she wanted to be? The fragile girl who *needed* a way out?

"I like him a lot," Kayla said, her tone maybe too serious. Maybe everything was too serious, but Liam wasn't exactly a joke. She didn't know *what* he was, but he wasn't that.

"Okay," Dinah said carefully.

"And there has been some dirty stuff."

Dinah let out a little whoop and crossed over and took Kayla by the shoulders. "Liam Patrick. Liam *Patrick*."

"Why do you keep saying his full name?" Kayla returned, laughing even harder as Dinah clapped her hands on Kayla's cheeks.

"I don't know. It's just *Liam Patrick*. We know him. He's our handyman. And, oh God, I'll never be able to look him in the eye again without wondering just how handy."

Kayla laughed even as she blushed all over again, and it was nice to laugh with Dinah, her cousin, her best friend. It was nice to be a little silly. But . . . "He's *Gallagher's* handyman, not ours."

Dinah's hands slipped off Kayla's face and she took a step back. "Right. Old habits." She smiled thinly.

Which wasn't what Kayla wanted either. She wanted to be brave, but she didn't want to lose . . . She wanted them to be *friends*, not Gallaghers. "He's very, very good with his hands," Kayla managed deadpan. "And his mouth."

Dinah all but choked on the gulp of wine she'd taken, but once she was done sputtering, she grinned. Dinah grabbed Kayla's free hand and led her out to the living room. They both settled in with their glasses of wine, a pan of brownies already on the table. Kayla had put two spoons next to the pan as was their old tradition.

"You have to tell me," Dinah said, leaning toward Kayla with a very serious expression on her face. "What size . . . tool are we talking about here?"

"Dinah!"

"If I don't know, every time I see him I'll *wonder*, and that's just not good for business."

"If we talk about Liam's tool, I'm going to start asking questions about Carter's . . ." Kayla struggled to come up with a farming-related term. "Cucumber!"

Dinah picked up a spoon, holding the wineglass regally in the other hand. She scooped out a bite of brownie and popped it into her mouth, chewing thoughtfully. "Carter's cucumber is very healthy. In fact, it might be the healthiest cucumber I've ever had."

Kayla burst into a fit of giggles and Dinah joined. This was nice. This was what she missed. Her friend over her coworker. Her cousin over her sharer-of-business-related interests.

"So, Liam's tool. Don't think you'll distract me with talk of my boyfriend's impressive cucumber."

"Impressive is a good word for it," Kayla managed, though she wanted to giggle some more. "Very, very impressive."

Dinah leaned back against the cushion and sighed dreamily as she sipped her wine. "A good man is hard to find. A good man who is also 'impressive' is *quite* the find. But you said you don't know what's going on."

Kayla frowned at her wine, then leaned over and took a big scoop of brownie. "I don't know why he lied. To you. About fixing a sink."

"Well, you know, I think he might have come here to unclog your drain."

Kayla rolled her eyes, but she couldn't help a smile. "There are too many metaphors going on. If a cucumber ends up in a drain, I think we're going to have problems."

Dinah opened her mouth, but then she shook her head and shoved brownie into it instead of saying anything.

Kayla frowned. "What?"

"Nothing."

"What were you going to say?"

Dinah sighed. "I was going to give you advice, and then I reminded myself you don't need it. You're a grownup, and I know half the reason you shut me out is because I didn't always treat you like one."

"No, it was because Gallagher's—" But at Dinah's raised eyebrow, Kayla realized Dinah had a point. She had framed it about needing space from Gallagher's, and Dinah's dedication to the family business meant that was her too, but it *had* been more than just business.

"Kay, I love you—*you*—not because of Gallagher's or because I used to boss you around and you'd listen, but because you're smart and you're kind and you've always known how to make me laugh, or very gently point out when I've gone a little off the deep end." Dinah leaned forward, eyes glistening with tears Kayla knew she wouldn't shed. "Things have changed for me since Carter. I'm not that same bulldozer. I don't want to be."

"Because of Carter?"

Dinah shrugged. "Kind of. I know I used to talk a big game about never letting a man change me or always feeling complete and happy without a boyfriend, and it's not like I've changed my mind on that, but . . . Love, well, it shifts your priorities, I guess. It makes you see things about yourself, good and bad, and I was in a kind of crappy place before Carter, and you know what? I'm not going to be ashamed to admit that meeting and falling in love with a really good guy who cares about me and wants to take care of me changed me a little bit. Fixed some things that were broken. Not all the things, sure, but some. Love is powerful. Even if that sounds lame, I don't care. I believe it. I lived it. I am living in that power and some days I want to smack that man so hard he sees stars, but I never, ever have regretted standing up to Grandmother and losing out on the director position. Even when he drives me to the brink of insanity, I don't want to be anywhere else."

Kayla wasn't quite sure what to do with that impassioned speech. It all made her vaguely uncomfortable. Love and good guys and all sorts of complicated things she wasn't all that certain she was strong enough for.

Besides, shouldn't she be happy with herself first? Shouldn't she know who she was without a shadow of a doubt before she started letting some guy change her? Dinah could say all that stuff because she'd always been strong. Kayla was still learning.

Not that Liam was . . . He was a good guy, and maybe he had taken care of her, but that's what he did. It had been a few hours over a few nights strung together. Dinah's speech shouldn't hit some weird place inside of her.

"Plus," Dinah continued, her smile going sly, "he's super-hot and really good at sex. That'll put anyone in a good mood."

Kayla managed a chuckle and decided to focus on that. On friendship. On brownies and wine and funny movies. On her best friend, who'd changed, and herself, who had too, and maybe tomorrow she'd know what to do about Liam Patrick.

But if she woke up as confused as ever, Kayla was certain of one thing: She wouldn't let that stop her.

Liam didn't go straight home from Kayla's. Instead, he'd dropped by his grandmother's house and she'd force-fed him the casserole she'd made for dinner.

She'd subtly mentioned how infrequent his visits were, and he took care of a few little projects. Changed a lightbulb that had gone out, oiled a squeaky door and the like.

He didn't even argue when she'd insisted on serving him dessert. He'd simply sat at her cramped dining room table and listened carefully to all her stories of his various cousins and their offspring.

God knew there'd be some kind of test to see if he'd been listening, and when he least expected it to boot.

Still, when he got up to leave, she'd patted his cheek and told him he was a "good boy." She'd given him that look that told him she had quite a few pieces of advice to bestow upon him but had decided to offer him reprieve tonight.

It had settled him, to be of some use to a person who mattered to him. To help, to fix, to listen. He didn't feel quite so churned up anymore.

At least until he pulled his truck into his usual parking spot on the street in front of his house. He frowned at the shadowy figure on his stoop. Even though he couldn't see the person, he had the sinking suspicion it was Aiden.

Which meant one of two things: Aiden was either in trouble or extraordinarily drunk. Maybe even both. But it was the only time Aiden ever came to Liam's place. Otherwise they only saw each other at Mom and Dad's when Aiden graced them all with his presence. But Aiden never let Mom see him drunk.

Liam had the insane urge to drive away. He didn't want to deal with Aiden's bullshit tonight. Not when he was still a little edgy underneath the calm that helping Grandma out had given him.

But Aiden was his brother, and if he was drunk or in trouble, it was Liam's duty to help. Like Dad had said earlier, Aiden just required a bit more attention, a bit more help. Liam didn't want Mom or Dad or, God forbid, Grandma having to worry about Aiden's shit.

So Liam got out of his truck and trudged toward his front door.

"Well, there you are," Aiden slurred, still just a dark shadow on Liam's stoop. "Don't tell me bro-bro has a life."

"Bro-bro? Christ, how drunk are you?" Liam muttered, taking the step up to the concrete pad.

Aiden stumbled to his feet. "Very, very, *very* drunk," he said gravely. "Where've you been, asshole?"

Liam sighed. "Grandma Patrick's house."

Aiden laughed. Hysterically. He even slapped his knee a few times as if Liam had just told the joke of the century. "Of course you fucking were. You were fixing her fucking toilet and probably vacuuming her fucking curtains and she gave you milk and fucking cookies. Saint fucking Liam."

"Isn't that something like blasphemy?" Liam replied drily. Clearly Aiden was itching for a fight, and Liam was not in the mood to navigate Aiden's mercurial temper when he was drunk.

But that was his job, wasn't it? And he'd learned a few tricks after thirty years on the planet. First, never rise to the bait Aiden laid.

Liam unlocked his door and shoved it open before motioning Aiden inside. "I suppose you want a place to crash."

"Nowhere else to go," Aiden muttered, weaving and stumbling into the house.

Liam flicked on a light and Aiden collapsed onto the couch.

Liam frowned, the first trickle of worry over annoyance skittering down his spine. It certainly wasn't the first time Aiden had shown up at his place drunk and antagonistic, but this was . . . extreme.

"Where have you been? Mom's been worried."

Aiden laughed again, though not quite as uproariously. "Do you ever fight your own fucking battles, Liam? Or are you always too busy taking up the sword for every damn other person."

"What the hell does that mean?"

"It means maybe if Mom is worrying it's none of your damn business."

"My brother. My mother. My *family.* That's my business, Aiden. Maybe you don't feel the same way, but—"

"But I'm wrong, right? I'm unfeeling and selfish and so fucking wrong?"

The worry buried deeper. Aiden usually didn't have a bad thing to say about himself. "What is with you?"

Aiden shrugged. "Everything, right? Isn't that what everyone's always saying? *I* am the problem. *I* am an asshole. A wolf in sheep-ass clothing."

"You're drunk enough to be incomprehensible. Sleep it off."

Of course, instead, Aiden pushed off the couch and weaved enough that Liam felt the need to reach out and steady him.

"'S fine," Aiden said, pushing Liam's steadying hand away. "I ended shit and it's all fine and dandy. I'll call Kayla tomorrow and everything will be fine."

Liam kept himself very still, reminded himself to breathe, to be the rational, sober adult in the room. Because a good half of that didn't make sense. "You're staying away from Kayla from here on out. Understood?"

Aiden squinted at him. "Says who?"

"Me."

"Lemme guess," Aiden said, apparently attempting to slap Liam on the shoulder but missing entirely. "You think she's too good for me."

"That's not—"

"Kayla Ganna—Gabba—*Gallagher* is a fucking princess and I am a useless fuckup."

"I didn't say that, Aiden," Liam said through gritted teeth. He didn't know what to do with his brother being a drunken, self-pitying ass. He could fight antagonism. He knew what to do with that.

In what seemed to be the theme for today, he did not know what to do with this.

"Don't have to say what's truth. But maybe someone good and shit would fix what's wrong with me."

"Only you can fix what's wrong with you," Liam replied flatly as Aiden plopped back onto the couch. He sprawled out and closed his eyes.

"You're confusing us, Li-Li. You're the strong one. *You* can fix everything. Well, 'cept me, but sometimes I wonder if you ever tried."

"Look, Kayla and I . . ."

But Aiden was making a faint snoring sound, his face lax, his body limp. Well, Liam supposed explanations about Kayla could wait until morning when Aiden was more likely to remember it anyway.

Liam shoved a cushion under his brother's head, hoping to God he didn't have to clean up another person's puke *again*. But he wondered if Aiden was right.

Maybe he'd never really tried to help Aiden. Maybe he'd only ever pushed him away.

Chapter Eleven

Kayla was sick with nerves, which wasn't all that uncommon in her life, really, but it was uncommon when it came to Liam.

Still, they hadn't exactly discussed . . . anything. They'd agreed to see each other tonight, but what did that mean? She didn't have a time, a place. All he'd done was fucking nod at her and repeat *tomorrow*.

She kind of wanted to punch him right about now.

Instead, she'd picked up a pizza at a place kind of close to his house, and she was going to be damn brave enough to march up to his door and offer dinner and sex. And if he turned her down, she'd live.

Maybe punch him too, but mostly she'd live.

But as she turned onto his street, his truck was parked where he always seemed to park it, which meant he was home. Probably.

Her stomach lurched and even the smell of pizza didn't help. Why was she doing this? What was the point of potentially embarrassing herself?

She looked at his little house and thought about his meticulously organized workshop, the way he'd kissed her last night, the scrape of his beard on her thighs.

Okay, well, there were some convincing arguments there. She grabbed the pizza and got out of her car. She breathed through the nerves as she walked up to his front door.

Embarrassment wasn't fatal. Feeling foolish would eventually fade, so she had everything to gain and nothing to lose. If she could only get that through to her churning stomach.

She stood on his porch and probably the only thing that eventually got her to knock on Liam's door was a man staring at her a little too intently from across the street.

It didn't take long for the door to swing open, and he must have looked out a peephole or something because he was smiling when he opened it. "Hey."

"Hi," she managed. "I hope I'm not . . . overstepping," she offered lamely, and then inwardly berated herself for it.

"Not at all."

Before she thought better of it, she reached out with her free hand and cupped his cheek, rubbing her thumb over the coarse texture. "You look tired."

His mouth curved in that world-weary way of his. "I was up half the night taking care of a drunk person."

"That's a nasty habit you have." Something like jealousy poked at her, though she didn't want to be *that* girl. But apparently she was. "Who?"

"Aiden."

"Oh." She felt unaccountably awkward at the mention of the brother she'd first agreed to go out with.

"It was . . . Well, you brought pizza. Come inside." He took the box from her and walked toward his kitchen. Kayla closed the door and followed him.

"Do you want to talk about it?"

He grabbed two plates from a cupboard. "Why?"

She studied him for a moment, coming to the conclusion he was well and truly baffled. That it would never occur to him to unload his problems on someone else. It was fascinating because she recognized that, though they came at it from different places.

She'd always been told by someone or another that her problems were less important, and so she'd learned to stuff them down. Liam seemed to take responsibility for everything, to hold that responsibility to himself because he felt as though it was his job to fix.

But maybe that came from a similar place. She'd been an avoider. He was clearly a fixer, but maybe it all stemmed from feeling like their own problems weren't worthy.

"Sometimes it feels good to tell someone what's bothering you."

He stared at the pizza as he seemed to puzzle over her words. Something in her chest pinched. Maybe her heart. She wanted . . . She *wanted* him to tell her what was wrong, and she wanted to offer him some comfort.

"It is what it is." He squared his shoulders and smiled at her. "I'll fix it." So certain and sure.

"You'll fix what exactly?" she pressed, and then wondered why she *was* pressing when she could be eating pizza or having sex or *not* talking about his brother who'd asked her out not all that long ago.

His eyebrows drew together and he moved his gaze to her as if the question didn't make sense.

"Aiden isn't an it, any more than he's someone who's your job to fix," she said gently.

"He's my brother."

"Yes." Kayla accepted the plate he'd handed her and took her time taking a bite of pizza. "You know, I've spent the time since I stood up to my grandmother and father and quit waiting for something to happen. I did the hard part. I stood up to them, and the world was supposed to reward me with some grand sign or gesture."

He didn't say anything, and she took another bite of pizza while trying to organize her thoughts. "But in the end, the world couldn't magically give me what I wanted. I had to . . . Don't you see? Six months ago, I never would have shown up here with a pizza. I never would have gotten drunk and insisted on coming to your workshop. I would have retreated into some safe place, no matter that I had been told my whole life that that's what I did. *I* had to decide I didn't want to be that anymore."

"He stood—okay, well laid there—and told me I fixed things, but I never . . ." Liam stopped talking, shaking his head and looking away from her.

And clearly this was not some misunderstanding, some little blip in his relationship with his brother, but something far bigger, because Liam held his jaw tight, his eyebrows furrowed, and though outwardly he looked stoic, Kayla thought there was a vulnerability in that stoicism.

She sat her plate down on the counter and crossed to him, placing her palms on his chest. "He said you never what?"

Liam's blue gaze met hers for the briefest second, but he didn't hold it, so she couldn't be sure it was a naked hurt that had lingered in their depths. "He said I'd never even tried to fix him."

Kayla shook her head. "That isn't your job."

He was silent for a while, but she noted something that maybe shouldn't have brought her pleasure, though it did. He didn't step away from her hands, didn't push them away. In fact, as she rubbed them up and down his chest in what she hoped was a comforting gesture, he even seemed to breathe a little easier.

"Why are we talking about this?" he asked, a forced smile curving his mouth but not reaching his eyes.

Still, she smiled up at him, because she didn't know the answer. This wasn't exactly what she'd come for, and still . . . She wanted it. Those moments of getting to know a person, because she was finally brave enough to open up to that instead of shy away from it. "I don't know."

His fingers brushed over the hair that waved over her shoulders, rubbing the ends of a few strands between his thumb and forefinger. His gaze moved from her hair to her face, and everything inside of her mind went totally blank.

He was just so handsome, and . . . He was something she struggled to define. Not fierce, exactly, but something more dazzling than sturdy and sure.

Slowly, stretching out the moment until it was nothing but vibrating anticipation, his mouth lowered closer to hers. When his lips finally touched hers, feather light, sweet and seductive, it had the power of a gunshot. Loud and disorienting, a bolt of feeling that was so sweet it was almost painful.

And that was all the kiss was. A brief, sweet thing that left her shivering and desperate for more, especially with his mouth still so close to hers.

"I like you," she blurted out, feeling somehow half brave and *right* and half embarrassed beyond belief.

But his smile shifted from that fake, blank thing it had been before to something warm and exciting. "I like you too," he said in his low gravelly voice, his hands sliding over the backs of hers, still on his chest.

She had to look down, to swallow at the way that waved through her, strong and potent. It even made her throat a little tight, but it also made her think of last night. "So why'd you lie to Dinah?"

"I don't know. There was an awkward silence, and I just . . ." His fingers curled around her hands, but he didn't remove them from his chest. He just held them there. "I thought maybe you didn't want to tell her. Or maybe you didn't want anyone to know."

She forced herself to be the brave, take-a-stand woman she

wanted to be in this . . . relationship. "I don't care who knows," she said firmly.

He inclined his head. "Okay."

They stood there, for she wasn't sure how long, just staring at each other. She'd come here and he'd welcomed her. She'd broached an uncomfortable subject and they'd talked it out.

But she was done talking. She slid her hands up his chest, his hands falling to his sides as she wrapped her arms around his neck and tugged his mouth down to hers. They'd talked and shared and opened up to feelings, but she wanted different feelings now.

She didn't want to talk about how she felt. She wanted to show him. So she pressed her mouth to his, outlined his lips with her tongue. She curled her fingers in his thick hair and poured every ounce of herself into that kiss.

He banded his arms around her, pulling her so close she could feel his erection against her belly. She pressed against it, satisfied at the groan that emerged from the back of his throat. She wanted him desperate and needy for her. The way she was for him at something as simple as that little whispered kiss.

She scraped her teeth across his bottom lip and he pressed her firmly against the counter behind her. She tried to angle her hips, to rub herself against him, but he was so much taller and broader and stronger, she didn't have any leverage.

But leverage didn't matter with his mouth hot on hers, his beard abrasive and wonderful against her chin.

He tugged her shirt up and as they had to break contact she realized neither of them had eaten very much. "Oh, the pizza . . ."

"Is microwavable. I want to be inside you, Kayla." He paused for a second, his mouth a whisper away from hers. He cleared his throat. "You, uh, can tell me not to say stuff like that."

"I like it." She nipped at his bottom lip, gratified when he grinned that rare, wolfish grin. Like she could tug down that capable, unfazed facade, just as he tugged down her timid, *fragile* one.

His hands slid down her arms and then his fingers curled around her wrists. She was pressed up against the counter and he wasn't just caging her in. He held her hands behind her against the counter so she couldn't move her arms.

And then he sighed with something very close to disgust in his expression. "I left the condoms at your place last night."

* * *

Liam was ready to drag Kayla right out the door and head to her apartment. Or maybe a drugstore would be closer, but something about the way Kayla grinned at him made him pause.

"What do you take me for?" she asked, wiggling out of his grasp and grabbing the purse she'd set down. She rummaged around in the bag that was pink and about the size of her head before she pulled out the box of condoms he'd dropped at her place last night.

She looked so pleased with herself, self-satisfied and easy with it, nothing like the woman he'd seen her as not that long ago.

It was kind of amazing he got to see this side to her, because she hadn't always been that free and easy with it. Maybe it was part of the new path she was blazing, but maybe it had something to do with him. Or them together.

"You do come prepared," he managed to say, keeping himself from rubbing at the weird tightness in his chest.

"We've had a few things interrupt us. I wasn't about to let that happen again."

"Come here." Because if she didn't come to him, he was liable to lose whatever locks he had on the control it took to keep from simply taking her to the floor and ending this all too quickly. He had no qualms about the floor, but he wanted more than quick and reckless.

God help him.

She arched an eyebrow at him. "In the kitchen?" she returned skeptically.

He returned the arched eyebrow look. "I think we can do it anywhere we want."

She ran a finger under the top of the box, carefully pulling it open. She pulled one condom out of it before walking slowly toward him. Not even a walk. She downright sauntered, and Liam stood where he was watching Kayla Gallagher walk across his kitchen straight for him. Him.

She held out the condom. "You're in charge of that."

He took it from her, and though he wanted to immediately touch her, *take* her, he simply placed the condom in his pocket and waited. He was too curious to see what her first move would be. Would she be bold? Shy? Would she do that shoulders back, deep breath thing where she mustered up all of her courage and did something clearly out of the ordinary for her?

The funny thing was, he liked all of those parts of her. The shy and the brave. The timid and the bold. All of it made up this woman standing before him, and he was so damn gone over her he could barely see straight.

She reached out and brushed her fingertips over his beard. It never failed to send a shudder through him. She did it when she wanted to comfort him, like when they'd been talking about Aiden. She did it when they kissed. She did it and it was always a certain level of sweet to feel someone reach out and touch him so gently.

It was a . . . rarity. So much of one he didn't even realize it was rare until she did it. He supposed that was his own fault, as gruff and quiet as he could be. Still, it didn't seem to faze Kayla.

Though he'd meant to wait and see what her next move would be, he placed his hand over hers on his jaw, unable to resist connection over connection.

"You like it when I do that?" she asked softly.

"Yes."

"Do you like having a beard?"

He laughed at the odd question. "Well, yes, that is why I have it. Do you like it?"

She grinned and nodded. "I've never dated a guy with facial hair before." Her eyebrows drew together. "I guess technically we're not dating."

"I . . ." He didn't know what to say to that. They hadn't exactly been on any dates. He should probably rectify that. She definitely deserved dates in nice restaurants and, like, art places or some shit. Stuff she was interested in. He should be trying to impress her, and instead they were always at his place making out in his kitchen.

Which truth be told was *his* preference, but this wasn't all about him.

"I didn't mean to make it weird. It's not like we have to date. I . . ." She shook her head and did that squared shoulders thing. She opened her mouth, likely to say something more confident sounding, but he didn't want to let that awkward silence stand enough for her to be the one who had to fix it.

"I guess we haven't been on an official date, but it's not like we're not seeing each other."

"Seeing each other," she repeated and she smiled.

"But we can. I mean we will. Date. And . . . shit." He closed his eyes feeling like a tool. "Can we go back to the precursor to sex, because I'm fairly confident in my skills there. Talking, not so much."

She rubbed her hand up and down his jaw again, and Liam never took his hand off of hers. He just followed the movement.

"I think you do okay," she offered, her mouth still that sweet curve, her hand a gentle, comforting pressure against his face.

"If that's actually true, it's because of you, because no one has ever given me credit for being good with words. Unless they were to break up a fight."

She bit her bottom lip, looking at him through those golden lashes. There was something in her expression he couldn't read. "Ever the fixer."

She didn't say it with awe or gratefulness, not an ounce of Aiden's sarcasm. She said it as if it were simply an inexorable part of himself, and he'd always thought *that* was true. Fixing wasn't a choice he made. It was simply who he was.

Still, he didn't know what that meant with Kayla. She needed none of his fixing, and somehow that was both terrifying and . . . tempting.

Something good and bright and sweet, all for him. He didn't have a clue what to do with that, so he lowered his mouth to hers. He tried to give her some semblance of what he felt in the kiss. Sweetness and hope. A chest-tightening, heart-pinching, brain-defying feeling that was all gentle brushes and light pressure.

Her fingers moved up over his cheeks and his temples and into his hair. She melted against him soft and sweet and pliant.

For the first time in all the ways they'd come together, he felt content to take things slow. To run his hands over her neck, feeling each goose bump pop up. To memorize the slope of her shoulders and the soft texture of her inner wrist. To mold his hands over her sides and hips and commit them to a memory of more than just brain, but soul and heart.

She sighed into his mouth, and though his dick throbbed with the need and want, his heart pounded slowly and contentedly to exist here in the sweet honey taste of her mouth and the velvety softness of her lips. He was happy to exist in this moment of perfection.

Until she gave his hair a little tug. Hard enough to pull his mouth a fraction away from hers. His eyes fluttered open and he glanced down at her. She had a flush to her cheeks and her lips were wet from his mouth and tongue. Her eyes were dark metallic blue and everything about her was a study in perfect beauty.

She didn't say anything and for a few seconds they simply looked at each other, his heart beating hard against hers.

She released his hair slowly, and then her fingers dipped under his shirt and she tugged the hem up with a slow, almost agonizing pace. Her fingertips explored the expanse of his stomach, back and forth and up and down until he practically had to shudder with the need for more. But she only laughed and moved higher, his shirt lifting only as far as her arms did.

Her fingertips missed nothing. They moved feather light over the ridge of his stomach, moving across the indentations of his chest. She scraped her fingernails across his nipples and he choked back a moan. All the while she watched the path of her fingers, grinning. It was that grin, that self-satisfied smirk he only just learned she had, that kept him from stopping her or doing anything in return.

She pulled the shirt up over his head and dropped it onto his kitchen floor. He supposed another man would give Kayla candlelight and flowers and bedrooms and something that made sense, something that fit her grace and beauty. But he couldn't find it in him in this moment to offer those things to her. He wanted her. Her hands on him, her body bared to him. He didn't particularly care what kind of lighting there was or what room in his house they were in. He just wanted her.

Her fingertips scraped down his chest and stomach to the button of his pants. She began to unfasten his jeans, tugging them down. With every move she made, she carefully avoided the thick protrusion of his erection. She was teasing him and something about that struck him as perfect.

But when she began to lower to her knees, he grabbed her hard and quick to stop her. "No."

She looked up at him with something like a pout. "But I want to taste you."

Christ, she was going to kill him. "There will be very few times in my life where I say no to that, Kayla, but tonight I want . . . I need . . ." He thought back to earlier when he'd said the crude words to her. And she'd said she liked it.

"You want to be inside me," she said, not quite meeting his gaze.

"I *need* to be inside you."

She bit her lip again. "Well . . ." She glanced up at him, her smile spreading. "That can probably be arranged, but you might have to take off my clothes."

He laughed, though it came out more of a strained chuckle. But he didn't reach out to take off her clothes.

Maybe it was foolish to want this to be special. He'd never been any good at making things special. Romantic. That just wasn't who he was, but when it came to Kayla, he wanted to be able to find it in himself to give her something special or important. He wanted to show her that even though he could be rough and not very good with softness, he did have it in him. When it came to her.

Which was probably stupid.

"Okay, I'll do it myself." She pulled her shirt up and over her head, dropping it on top of his on the floor. She reached back presumably to undo her bra, but he put a hand on her soft stomach, splaying out his fingers to revel in the velvety satin of her skin.

"Stop," he ordered. He needed to get in the game. Focus. Stop worrying about "special" and shit like that and enjoy the damn moment.

She cocked her head as if considering whether or not to listen to him. "You know, as much as I like your orders, and believe me I definitely do, I think tonight . . ." She nodded her head as if she'd made some important decision. "Tonight I'm going to be in charge. And I'll take very good care of you," she whispered, kissing his chest right above where his heart thudded hard.

It was meant to be about sex, but in the context of this night and her asking him what was wrong, and *listening* to his problems, it felt so much more weighted.

People didn't *take care* of him. Why would they? He could take care of himself.

"Not so used to that, are you?" she asked, brushing her mouth against his jaw.

"Which part?"

She chuckled. "Both, I think. Not used to being taken care of, and not used to letting anyone else be in charge. Well, I think it's time you experience both."

"Do you now?"

She moved onto her toes, pressing a firm kiss to his mouth. "Yes," she said, meeting his gaze, so sure and beautiful. "Prepare yourself for total domination."

He raised an eyebrow at that and the pink flush of excitement on her cheeks turned darker, closer to red.

"Okay, maybe domination wasn't the right word," she said, her voice ending on a squeak.

He laughed and he couldn't remember ever laughing with someone over sex. Couldn't ever remember feeling this lightness along with all of the hammering need and heat.

There was a little prickle of unease at the back of his spine. The concern this was too much for him. Too big. He would ruin it.

He shoved that thought away, because he was not a ruiner. He was a fixer.

Chapter Twelve

Kayla had never seduced a man before. Of course, this wasn't exactly seduction. Liam was already seduced. He wanted to have sex with her. He was quite ready to have sex with her. This was about her taking charge.

She had definitely never, ever done that before. She had always let the guy lead, and there was something nice about that, but she wasn't looking for *nice* here. She was looking for important and meaningful. She felt both of those things because not only was she doing something she'd never done, but she was giving him something he'd never had.

She rubbed her palms over the hard plane of his chest. He was so broad. Muscle and hair and just so very . . . manly, she supposed. Which seemed like a silly descriptor, but she'd never met someone who had that sort of virility. She didn't know anyone who fixed things and made things, who seemed to take care without steamrolling over everything.

She'd never known anyone like him. So she kissed him and touched him. She reveled in the slow, soft way he touched her back as if giving her the thing she wanted. The power. The control. He was touching her only in the ways she touched him. Giving her the space to lead.

She arched against him, rubbing what she could against the hard long length of him. He was so very big. He would fill her completely.

Maybe she was setting herself up for disappointment, but she had a feeling that finding her orgasm wouldn't be the struggle it usually was. Usually it was a lot of trying to figure out how to contort herself without having to tell the guy he wasn't quite hitting the right spot.

But Liam . . . He seemed to be able to look at people and understand them. She was probably putting too much faith in that, but with the promise of sex, it was hard to care. It was hard to worry.

They would work together to get them both to that final part, of that she was sure.

Slowly she drew her mouth from his, looking up at him and studying the hard lines of his face. He looked so very serious and yet there was something sort of . . . lighter about him. Sometimes he had the world-weary heaviness about all the things he took care of, but he'd dropped that somewhere along the line tonight.

It was almost as if *she* had caused that in him. Maybe he liked her that much, and her presence was something like meaningful. Not a pretty decoration, not someone to manipulate. Just someone he enjoyed being with.

She took his hand in hers, determined to make this . . . special. It was probably schoolgirl foolishness that she wanted her first actual sex time with Liam to be *special*—something she could remember and cherish, but that's exactly what she wanted from this. From him.

But if she thought too much about that, tried too hard for that, it would lead to another hundred thoughts that were probably too serious for where they were right now. So she pushed them away and led Liam out of the kitchen, into the hall, and to his bedroom.

She didn't know why leading him gave her such a thrill. Obviously he was letting her do it and yet she didn't think he would let just anyone lead him.

Inside his bedroom, they stood facing each other. Him in only his low-slung jeans, and her in only her skinny jeans and bra.

She studied him and then his unmade bed. She felt giddy and nervous and one million other things at once, but mostly she knew that even if she said something silly or stupid, Liam would never make her feel those things. It was that which gave her the courage to be brave.

"Take off your pants and lay down."

His mouth quirked into a little bit of a smile, but he undid the button of his jeans, and then the zipper. He took the condom out of his pocket and tossed it onto the corner of the bed, then pushed his pants off his narrow hips and onto the ground. He aimed that lazy half-smile at her as he slid onto the bed, sprawling out on his back and crossing his arms behind his head.

He made quite the picture, all defined muscle at rest, impressive bulge under the boxers he wore.

She undid the clasp of her bra and let it fall to the ground. She didn't miss the way his mouth firmed and his eyes zeroed in on her naked breasts. She tried to memorize the way he breathed deeply and clearly appreciated the look of her as much as she appreciated the look of him.

Heart pounding, a steady thrum of need working through her body, she shimmied out of her own pants and stepped out of them so they lay on the floor next to his.

Willing herself to continue to be brave, she crawled up on the bed and over Liam. The soft slide of her legs against the coarse hair on his. She kept her hands on the smooth cotton of his sheets even as she let her gaze take in every last inch of him. Honed muscle and dark hair. The dips and curves of a man whose body was a tool he used at work.

Eventually her gaze traveled to his face. He still had that firm, jaw-tightened expressed about him, as though he had to fight that hard to hold himself back. Kayla couldn't say she minded if he did. His eyes were that glittering blue that should remind her of icy winter skies, but instead reminded her of the inside of a flame. His dark beard and hair such a sharp contrast to the color of his skin.

He didn't move underneath her, just looked right back at her. The only hint he felt anything was the tenseness of his jaw and the slightly heavy breathing.

The only place they touched was their legs, hers straddling his. Still, he didn't move to touch her, to bring her closer, and the moment stretched quiet and heavy, and somehow the pulsing need inside of her thudded harder, coiled tighter.

Was he wondering where she would touch him first? Anticipating it as much as she was? Their bodies coming together, fully, *wholly*. The thought ricocheted through her, hot and potent, so she lowered her body on top of his, stretching over him, every part of her touching him, except where they both still had on their underwear. His skin was surprisingly smooth in places, though rough against her chest and stomach where a smattering of hair rubbed against her.

She pressed a chaste kiss to his mouth, reveling in the feel of the hard outline of him through the thin cotton they both wore. Thick and ready. She wanted to tease him, maybe even torture him with that slight separation between them, but resting the already slick folds of herself against his cock was torture to her as well. She didn't want fabric barriers. She wanted him inside. Thrusting and hard and unrelenting.

She wanted so much more than a few gentle teasing touches. She wanted to be consumed by this strong, tough man.

And shouldn't she have what she wanted? What did special matter if it wasn't what she actually wanted? What did it matter what she was *supposed* to like or want when it came to sex? It was just the two of them. This would always just be for the two of them, and it didn't matter what was good or right or bad or wrong. It was only what she and he wanted.

She tugged the waistband of his boxers down and sighed at the gorgeous sight of aroused male. She slid her entire body down him as she pulled the boxers off his legs. She let her nipples brush against his thighs and her fingertips slide against his calves. She tossed the boxers away and then wriggled out of her own panties.

She grabbed the condom he'd placed at the corner of the bed. She didn't look at his face, afraid she'd lose her leading nerve. Instead, she focused on climbing back over him and slowly rolling the condom onto his erection.

She positioned herself over him, Liam still laying sprawled out with his hands behind his head. When she finally got the nerve to look at his face, he had such a smug expression she couldn't help but grin at him.

She held his gaze and that grin as she lowered herself onto him. Slowly, agonizingly having to let herself get used to the thick invasion. His grin died, turning into something harsher. She reveled in that look, the hot push of his cock, this slow, satisfying joining. His hands clamped on her hips and it sent another thrill through her. He'd lost the tacit agreement not to touch first, and she was more than excited that she'd moved him beyond that point.

Still, he didn't guide or stop her with his heavy grip. He merely put his hands there. Hard and big and rough. She found herself completely seated on him, her body desperate for more, and her brain function basically nonexistent. Heart hammering in her chest, she swiveled her hips slightly. When Liam groaned as though she'd caused him physical pain, she could only laugh.

Because no matter what happened here, she wasn't fully in charge. She had some power, and so did he. It was a partnership, an equal meeting.

She slowly moved, drawing him out and then deep again. She set a slow, steady pace, finding the exact angle she needed to hit that bright center of pleasure. She drew her fingers over his chest, and one of his hands slid from her hip, up her waist, and over to her breast. He teased rough fingertips over her nipples until she was panting at the electric bolts that went through her every time. As though every touch of her nipples was connected to that place where they met. Every brush of his fingertips across her skin bringing her closer to the orgasm she usually had to fight so hard for.

Liam was proving to be everything she'd wanted and hoped. Capable and sensitive, and maybe just wonderful. He never tried to rush her or slow her down. He simply touched her. Featherlight brushes, the ragged exhale of his breath at her shoulder.

And then it was more insistent, drawing her taut nipples between two fingers, a little bit of pressure. It was bigger and better and yet, no matter how close she felt, no matter how much she moved against him, it seemed as though her orgasm was just out of reach.

In the past, she would've given up. Faked it or just accepted that it wasn't going to happen this time. But this was Liam, and there was something more to this. An intimacy she'd never had, and she wasn't quite sure how it had come about, only that it was here. So she damn well wanted to orgasm around him.

Which meant she had to speak, and ask, and try to demand something better. She was in charge after all. In control. He'd given her that, and she was giving him that, too. Which meant she had to be brave enough to hold it with both hands and actually do it.

"Talk," she ordered a little roughly.

If he was surprised, he didn't show it. In fact, some of the tenseness seemed to leave his face, and his hands went from the glorious fondling of her breasts back down to her hips. That branding, clamping grip that made her catch her breath.

"You like fucking yourself on my cock, Kayla?"

And it was like lightning—heat and fire. Those dirty words, the rough way he said them, that deliciously mischievous look in his eye.

"More," she panted.

"You like me so deep inside you." He made a sound in the back of his throat, thrusting up to meet her and she groaned. "Yeah, you do. Lean forward."

She almost pointed out she was supposed to be in charge, but this was too amazing to argue with. She gave into it. She leaned forward.

"I want your sweet tits in my mouth." And with no exertion at all he reached up, all muscle and strength, and traced his tongue across her nipple.

She squeaked and jerked a little bit and somehow that was lightning too. Hitting a new spot inside of her. Liam held her still then, and pushed into her.

"You need it hard, baby. My cock pounding into you. Come on, baby, come. Come all over my cock, Kayla. So I can feel it."

God. God. She moved frantically against him as he pounded into her. He said her name like a prayer, begging her to come all over him. She supposed it was her name or that *please* that unwound all of the tightness inside of her.

One last hard thrust and that heartbeat of need pulsed through her. A sharp wave of pleasure and delight. Light and ecstasy even as he swore sharply and pushed deeper inside of her, making it all burst that much brighter. She collapsed against him, breathing heavily, her heart pounding and everything in her body a wonderful, pulsing electricity.

He kissed her temple, brushing the hair off of her face. His arms moved around her, holding her against him as though her weight was nothing. Still inside of her.

She sighed dazedly, contentedly burrowing into him. He brushed his fingers down her spine, a lazy, comforting gesture.

She wasn't sure how long they laid there before he finally suggested they go eat the pizza, but she would've been content to stay forever. That was certainly something she'd never, ever felt with a guy after sex—even good sex.

Kayla was beginning to realize that this whole "feeling new and different things with Liam" wasn't just her new leaf. It was him. It was them together. It was something big and special.

Which was terrifying, actually, and yet Kayla didn't want to be the girl who ran away from terrifying anymore. Which meant she had to hold on to it.

* * *

Liam woke up the next morning to the smell of something pretty. Flowery or citrusy or something. Whatever it was, it was definitely not a scent he was used to having in his house.

Even before he could convince himself to open his eyes, he could imagine bright red hair across his pillowcase. His mouth curved.

He opened his eyes, wanting to see it for himself. Wanting to stamp it into his memory, and he wasn't disappointed. Kayla's red hair was waving around not just her pillowcase, but his. A tangle of a crown of something very close to sunlight.

That chest-tightening thing that seemed to happen so often with her tried to steal his breath, but he inhaled and exhaled through it. Because she was here, and she liked him. They worked well together. So whatever was freaking him out a little bit, well, it was worth it, he supposed. She was something worth moving toward and fighting for.

He tried not to shift so she wouldn't wake up, but he rubbed his jaw against one of the strands of hair close to him. Yes, this was in fact something special and quite intimidating. He wasn't sure he could remember ever wanting something to work out quite so much. There were a lot of things in his life he'd hoped for, and he'd made them all happen. This wasn't going to be any different.

He glanced at his clock over her head. He would need to get up soon. He was supposed to meet Dad for coffee before their eight o'clock client.

Kayla shifted her body, rolling to her side so her back was to him, her ass brushing up against his already hardening dick.

He really didn't have time to give any attention to that. At all. The one time he'd been late to work because of her had to be a one-time-only thing. He couldn't let it become a habit. He was the responsible one.

She moved again, and this time he realized it was purposeful. She was rubbing her ass against his cock. All those thoughts about being responsible and on time just sort of died.

"Keep rubbing your ass against me like that and you're going to be very, very sorry."

Kayla laughed, the sound sleepy and muffled. "I really don't think sorry is what I'm going to be."

She rolled toward him, her eyes dark half-opened, her mouth curved and happy. She was one of the most beautiful women he'd ever seen. There was no way he would survive without taking her right now.

He found her hands under the covers and circled his fingers around her wrists, pulling them up and above her head as he angled himself over her. He used his knees to nudge her legs apart. He looked down at her like the feast she was. "Very, very sorry," he managed with as much mock seriousness as he could.

She grinned, sassy and hot. She arched up against him, the naked apex of her thighs just barely brushing the hard length of his dick.

He reached over to the nightstand and grabbed a condom from the box there. He tore the package open and pulled out the condom, rolling it on. Without preamble or foreplay, he simply entered her, her wrists still under his hand above her head.

Kayla groaned, opening her legs wide for him. She was wet and ready, perhaps even desperate for him, and it made him a little wild. A lot wild. He thrust once, hard, all the way inside of her.

"Fuck," she said on a ragged breath. That coarse word from her beautiful mouth was like some kind of starting pistol. He couldn't hold himself back. He withdrew and thrust. Hard and relentless, adjusting the angle until she gasped in pleasure every time he pushed hard into her.

She tugged her hands out of his grasp and grabbed at his hips, her nails sinking into his ass. Begging him, urging him faster.

"Harder," she breathed, and it was all he could do to keep himself from losing it right there as she begged him for more.

He leaned forward, still thrusting deep, groaning against her as he scraped his teeth across her nipple. She cried out.

"I love the way you look underneath me," he muttered, not even paying attention to what words were rushing out of his mouth. "My cock in your beautiful pussy. You're just about to come all over me, aren't you?"

"Yes, yes. I'm so close."

And so was he. Too close. "Touch yourself."

Her eyes widened and she looked right at him, a little panicked. She inhaled sharply, and if he'd had any brainpower left he might've slowed things down or told her not to worry about it, but instead he just watched her, never stopping his steady pace of sliding his cock deep inside her tight heat, the excruciating withdrawal, only to do it all over again.

She withdrew her hand from where it had clamped on to him. Though there was a slight tremor in her fingers, she bit her lip as she drew a finger over her own nipple. The timid way she touched herself just about killed him, but he gritted his teeth together and forced himself to last.

"That's not where I meant, Kayla."

Her cheeks that had already been flushed pink turned a darker shade. On another hitching breath, she lowered her hand down her stomach, pausing only once before she finally placed it against the top of her pussy. He watched her finger as he entered and withdrew from her. Each little brush of her finger was timid at first, but he watched the pleasure streak over her face as she got closer to her clit.

"Beg me," he ground out through shattering breaths. He wanted to lose himself inside her, let the heat and release wash over him.

"Fuck me, please," she whispered, still touching herself, her eyes dark and unfocused. "Harder, please. Please."

Then he was gone as he watched her touch herself, spasming deep inside of her as she sobbed out her own release. His sight went a little dim and his breathing was rough and ragged as the pleasure spiraled through his entire body, bright and intense.

"Well," he managed, once he caught his breath and collapsed onto his back next to her. "That's one way to start a morning."

She laughed, the sound rough and breathless. "I do have a job interview in a few hours. Maybe it'll be a good luck charm."

He turned, pulling her next to him as he nuzzled into her neck. "There was nothing not good luck about that."

"You know, if you have to go fast again so you won't be late, you can always leave me your key again and come pick it up after work."

"Are you trying to lure me to your apartment and have your dirty way with me?"

"Oh, yes. One hundred percent."

He grinned against her neck and tried to come to grips with how *happy* he felt. When was the last time he'd let himself have that? This deeply. This much just *his*. He thought it had to have been before Dad's heart attack, if that.

There were things a guy who was better with words could say to her to show her that, but he didn't have them. He had only himself, and he could only hope that would be good enough.

"I do actually have to get going. Dad wanted to have coffee before our first call."

"Go have coffee with your dad. And then I'll see you tonight?"

He nodded, forcing himself to get out of bed and head for the bathroom. He ran through the shower and got dressed for the day. He was running a little bit late, but hopefully Dad wouldn't mind if they rescheduled the coffee.

When he got back out of the bathroom, Kayla was still curled up in his bed. She was typing something into her phone. She smiled over at him.

"I was just teasing about me staying here while you go. It's probably weird having me in your house alone, and—"

He cut her off by placing his mouth on hers and kissing her. When he pulled away, she grinned at him.

He hurried to the kitchen and pulled his house key off his key ring and went back to the bedroom to hand it to her. Still naked in his bed. No, it somehow wasn't weird at all to leave her here. It was something like perfect.

"Stay. Make yourself at home. Eat my food, drink my coffee. Good luck at your interview. I expect to hear all about it tonight. At your place."

"I'll be waiting."

He indulged in one last kiss, groaning as he forced himself to end it and walk out the bedroom. He had work, no matter how much he'd rather play hooky.

And wasn't that damn weird? No matter whom he'd been seeing or sleeping with, he'd never been all too interested in giving up work for time spent with them.

He drove to his parents' house, belatedly realizing he'd forgotten breakfast or coffee, so high he'd been on sex and Kayla. He glanced at his clock, wondering if he and Dad would have time to grab something before they went over to fix Mrs. Washington's unhinged door.

But as he walked into his parents' house, happy and content, it all disappeared in an instant when he entered the kitchen to find his parents sitting at the kitchen table, hand in hand, looking all too grave.

"What is it?" Liam asked.

Mom had tears in her eyes, but Dad was the one who spoke. "Sit, son. We have to talk."

Which could not in any way, shape, or form be good.

Chapter Thirteen

Kayla knew it was silly to fuss. After all, Liam wasn't a fussy kind of guy. Still, *she* wanted to fuss and she had given herself permission to do something for herself even if Liam wouldn't particularly appreciate it.

So she hummed as she set the table. She'd bought some fresh vegetables at the orchard she'd interviewed at this morning and made a salad and some pasta, and had tried very, very hard not to think about how much she wanted the job.

So she focused all her energy on getting ready for Liam coming over and making it the perfect date-night-in kind of evening.

When the knock sounded at the door, her heart beat in extra time. Odd to be nervous, and yet this was still so new. No matter how he made her feel so comfortable, so brave or right, this was still like walking some kind of tightrope and holding her breath hoping she didn't fall off.

Because she so wanted to get to the other side.

She opened the door, nervous smile plastered on her face, but it immediately died. Liam looked . . . gray almost. His mouth drawn, shoulders drooped. He looked, quite frankly, like he'd been to hell and back.

"What's wrong?" she asked, immediately touching his arm and ushering him inside.

He moved, but he looked at her quizzically. "How do you know something is wrong?"

"You look . . ." Telling him he looked terrible was maybe not the kindest route to take, but then again Liam didn't exactly need kind. Or maybe he did. Maybe kind and care was exactly what he needed if no one saw him looking like this and asked him what was wrong. "What is it?"

He shook his head. "It's nothing."

"It's something," she said, firmly leading him to the couch. She pushed him until he sat down.

"It's . . . something that will be fine." He pulled her to sit next to him and then dropped a kiss to her mouth, but she found that no matter if she should or not, she didn't want to let it drop.

"If it will be fine, then you can tell me what it is."

He studied her, and she didn't know what he saw, but she thought it might be good because he reached out and drew a strand of her hair through his fingers. He took a deep breath and released her hair and then offered the most pathetic smile she'd ever seen.

"My dad has to get a few stents."

"Stents. That's like for heart—oh, he had a heart attack a few years ago, didn't he?"

Liam nodded. "They did the whole bypass surgery, but I guess it's not doing quite what it's supposed to. They'll try stents first and if that doesn't work, they'll suggest surgery again. But . . ."

"But what?"

Liam shook his head. "It's all conjecture crap at this point. We do the stents first and see how it goes." He pushed off the couch, clearly agitated and not at all as Zen as he *wanted* to be about the whole thing. "I just . . . He says if he needs another bypass, he won't get it, but how do you do that? There's a fix and you're just going to say no?"

"But he's already had one, and it didn't fi—" She clamped her mouth shut at the horrified look on his face. She pushed off the couch too, willing herself to find a way to comfort him. "The first step is the stents. That's the most important thing."

He raked his hands through his hair. "It is. That's exactly what I told Mom, and I got her calmed down, at least for a while. And I'm sure the stents will work. He's done everything right. He . . ." He tensed his jaw, trailing off, clearly working through some heavy emotion before he pushed it away, blanking his expression. "Something smells very good."

He was so good at that, erasing that moment of pain that had been on his face. Changing the subject. She could almost believe that that's what he wanted. To move on and away, but he fancied himself such a *fixer* of things, and this was quite certainly something he couldn't fix.

It would be a blow, and she wondered if anyone in his life would see it? Or would they all be so worried about his father, and rightfully so, that they missed each other's stress and pain over it? Liam had calmed his mother, and probably done the work of two men today, and now he was here, and didn't he deserve somewhere he didn't have to be the fixer?

She crossed over to him where he stood looking very blankly at the kitchen. His gaze didn't move to hers, but she didn't let that deter her. She wrapped her arms around him, no matter that his were crossed over his chest.

"Everyone expects you to be the rock, don't they?"

He was so still, utterly stone-like for the longest minute, and then ever so slowly his head moved against hers. A very minor nod, but a nod nonetheless.

She squeezed her arms tighter around him. "I can be your rock for a little bit," she whispered, because while she had often stood in the wake of Dinah's storms and shouts, offered encouragement here and there, being a *rock* was never needed. Dinah was her own force. Dad had never been anything other than cold and distant even before Mom had left.

Kayla had tried to comfort and always failed at it, but she wouldn't step back from Liam when she knew she could give him something.

Eventually, he uncrossed his arms and maneuvered so that he held her as she held him. His breathing wasn't quite even, and though she couldn't see his face because his cheek rested against her temple, she could feel a sort of crack in that stone-like veneer.

He cleared his throat. "I'm . . ."

She waited for the end of that sentence, but it never came. And she supposed if she were the rock, the caregiver, then she had to take a stab at the possible ending herself. Even if she was wrong. She'd always been so afraid of being wrong, maybe now it was time to be afraid of not doing *anything*. "Scared?"

He was silent for a long, drawn-out minute, and she held her breath, hoping he wouldn't walk away, offended or hurt she'd put that on him.

"Yes, that," he said gruffly.

"I think that's more than natural."

"But so is everyone else. Someone has to be brave. Someone has to say it'll be okay." Still, his arms tightened around her, strong and hurting.

"Why does it have to be you?"

"I don't know. It just always has been."

"How about this?" She pulled slightly back so she could look him in the eye. So she could give him something. *Something*. "For them, you can be what you always have been, but here, with me, you can be scared or unsure or whatever it is you need. And I'll be the strong and sure one."

He stared at her as though she'd spoken a foreign language. Some string of words he couldn't make sense of.

Maybe it didn't make any sense, but she was going to cling to the idea anyway. She reached up and rubbed her palm across his jaw, not just reveling in the rough texture of his beard, but also in the way he leaned into the touch.

He exhaled, then pressed his mouth to hers. Gentle and sweet, as though seeking something soft and comforting, not the rough, desperate kisses of last night. Nothing fun or purely sex. Gentle.

"I don't want to have to think about it," he said against her mouth.

"Then we won't." She cupped his face and kissed him, just as soft and gentle as the previous one, not letting herself hold anything back out of fear or nerves. She gave him all of the empathy and comfort and warmth and care and didn't let herself worry if it was too much or too soon.

Kayla was like a salve to a wound after his shit day. Nothing had unwound him after Mom crying all over him this morning, or Dad making it steadfastly known if the stents didn't work, he was done. No amount of fixing door hinges or unclogging drains or patching up roofs had given him a second of satisfaction or solace.

Kayla wrapping her arms around him, Kayla understanding, and her sweet mouth under his, it gave him acres of solace.

It still hurt like a bitch, all in all, but it was different. Not that wild, howling beast inside of him swirling and desperate to *do* something.

She'd tamed it. With her words, with her kiss. He felt utterly, happily reined in. Her hands cupping his cheeks, her soft body pressed against his. It was like some magic thing he'd been missing all these years.

Or she was.

"Kay." He didn't know what to say. There was this aching beat inside of him that only ever existed with her. She was this glorious wonderful light, and yet it hurt to look directly at that.

"Not very many people shorten my name," she murmured, touching the collar of his shirt, half her fingertip on the fabric and half tracing along his skin.

"Who constitutes 'not very many'?" he returned, because there was this stupid, immature need inside of him to be something special to her the way she was something special to him.

Her dark blue gaze met his and at the very least she looked just as serious as he felt. "Well, just Dinah really."

"Does that make it weird?"

She chuckled, her fingertips still moving back and forth across his shirt and skin. "You don't exactly sound like Dinah, Liam. I think I can work out the difference."

"I can think of a few ways to make sure of that," he returned, and though he'd been convinced he wouldn't feel much like company or even sex when he'd been on his way over here, now it was all he wanted. All he needed.

Except, shit. "I didn't bring over the condoms. I wasn't really thinking and—"

"I bought some for my place." She smiled up at him. "They're in my bedroom. Which is the first door on the left, if you were wanting to lead."

"You are . . ." Perfect, maybe.

"Always prepared? Like a Boy Scout."

"Yeah, something like that," he said, finding her grin infectious, finding everything about her irresistible. So he picked her up, gratified when she immediately wrapped her legs around him, which made it very easy to walk down her hallway.

"First door on the left, you said?"

She nibbled at his earlobe, fidgeting against him until he lowered her enough that she could rub herself against his dick. "That's it."

He toed the door open and stepped into a room. There was some light creeping through a few slats in the shades, but mostly it was dim.

"All right, Boy Scout, time to show me what else you're prepared for." He dumped her on the bed, everything about her breathless laugh brightening the dark room. She was sunshine itself.

He tugged his shirt over his head and kicked off his shoes. Kayla licked her lips and watched.

"I love the way you look," she said on a sigh as if she hadn't thought about the words before they tumbled out.

He raised an eyebrow at her and a faint pink crept across her cheeks.

"You're just h-hot."

He supposed it was that screwy thing inside of him that liked her stutter, and in any other situation it might have caused him to pause, but so far Kayla had liked or matched every screwy thing he'd wanted. So what was the point in stopping? "Am I?"

"Well, o-of course you are. You're so . . . tall."

"Tall?"

"A-and broad shouldered and . . . your eyes are . . ." She rolled her eyes. "Are you fishing for compliments, Liam Patrick? Because that doesn't seem like you at all."

"Maybe I am," he returned, sliding one knee onto the bed, and then the other, moving closer and closer to her, never once looking at anything but those pretty eyes widening at his advance, before dropping to the bulge in his jeans.

"What else do you like about me, Kayla?" he said, his voice something more like a growly scrape against the air.

The pink blush on her cheeks was turning much closer to red, and he liked that too because she was breathing heavily. He could see the hardened peaks of her nipples through her bra and shirt. He had no doubt that if he touched her she'd be wet and needy.

Fuck.

He took her hand and closed it over the erection in his pants. "Do you like my cock, Kayla?"

"Yes."

"And what do you want me to do with my cock?"

She inhaled sharply, but she didn't say anything for a few taut seconds. She simply met his gaze and searched his face, something like compassion etched into the softness of her cheeks and eyes. Like if she looked hard enough she could give him what he needed to take all of today's troubles away.

"Why don't you tell me . . . Why don't you tell me exactly what you want? What you need?" she said, her voice little more than a whisper. "I'm here for whatever it is, Liam. I'm here for you."

It was his turn to inhale in a sharp burst, to hold it there, too many emotions and feelings crashing inside of him. His skin too hot, too tight, his heartbeat too loud in his ears, nearly painful in his chest.

For him. She was here for him.

"Get the condom. Then get undressed." He hardly recognized his voice, a low, unearthly growl. He should pause and rein it in, tamp all the swirling desperation down, but she was moving so quickly. She grabbed a condom out of her nightstand and put it on the top surface, and then her clothes were practically flying off of her until she laid out on her bed, naked and beautiful—pale skin, gold-dusted freckles, the rosy pink of her nipples.

He tore at his own pants, tugging them off with no finesse. This was about him. She was here for him. *Him*. No matter that some dim martyr's voice in the back of his head tried to tell him to stop, he bulldozed forward, grabbing the condom and opening it. Rolling it on while she watched.

"I want you on your hands and knees."

Her breathing hitched, but it was the only outward reaction before she was rolling over, rising up on her knees and hands, that beautiful ass of hers tilted toward him. A beautiful display. For him, for him.

The curve of her ass, the little birthmark at that sweet dip in her spine. He slid his hands over both of her ass cheeks, reveling in the smooth, plump part of her before smoothing his hands down the backs of her thighs, then up the inner section, finding her pussy.

"You're so wet," he said on a rumbling groan, stroking his finger across the hot seam of her. All of this for him.

She was breathing so hard, a little tremor running through her body. "Please," she whispered before looking over her shoulder at him. "I need you, Liam."

And whether she knew it or not, that was the thing. The thing he craved and wanted. The thing that unlocked all his pain and uncertainty. He just needed her to need him, however that need came. It rooted him to earth. It made him feel whole.

He positioned himself at her entrance, rubbing the head of his cock up and down her. Slowly, wanting to savor the delicious first slide into her, he entered, fraction by fraction, kneading his hands in her ass.

She tried to wriggle against him, but this was about *him*, so he clamped his hands on her hips, nudged her legs farther apart with his knees, finding a way to keep her just off balance enough that he was in control.

He held firm, seating himself completely, and she pushed back against him, the arch of her back so deliciously sexy he wanted to reach forward and bite her. Instead he pulled back, teasing with little, minuscule thrusts, only the head of his cock inside the sweet folds of her pussy.

She kept trying to move, to push back on him, but he held her where she was, having to take what little he gave her.

"Liam."

Something like a plea, and he laughed. Somehow, he laughed and delighted in not giving her what she wanted. "If you keep squirming, I'm going to have to punish you." And he wanted to shove those words back in his mouth the second they fell out. At least until she spoke.

"What are you going to do, spank me?"

He nearly jerked with the hot force of those words. Spank her. His rough hand slapping against that soft, supple ass cheek.

He sucked in a ragged breath, exhaled. "Is that what you need?"

She didn't respond to his question, but she kept squirming against him and he supposed that was answer enough. He smoothed his palm over the curve of her ass, his dick practically pulsing with unspent need.

He shook, but somehow that didn't stop him. He withdrew his hand and then brought it back down with a slight smack across her ass.

"Fuck," she groaned.

And he couldn't help himself, he shoved hard, as far as he could move inside of her, leaning completely over her back until he could whisper in her ear. "I love it when that sweet little mouth says that dirty little word."

She tilted her head to the side as much as she could, and even though he couldn't make eye contact, he watched as her mouth moved quite resolutely.

"Fuck," she enunciated.

And that was it. He was done playing around. He gripped her hips again and began to *fuck* her. Hard thrusts and labored breathing and the promise of release roaring through his veins. His body was electric, all tightened ecstasy and frantic pounding.

She moaned, her head bent down and pressing into the mattress, her red hair sprawled around her. He pumped harder, wanting to elicit more of those unabashed groans of pleasure.

She threw her head back and pushed hard against him, coarse words and his name on her lips as she came around him, spasming and soaking up every last moment.

He wanted to come, needed to, but first he needed to see her face. To watch her, to be watched in return.

He withdrew completely and she whimpered as though it was some kind of loss, and that ricocheted through him like everything seemed to. "On your back." Surely too rough a command and yet she scrambled to obey.

She spread her legs wide, an invitation, and he pushed home without a second's hesitation. Her eyes fluttered closed, but it wasn't what he wanted. "Look at me, Kayla. Watch me come."

Her blue eyes latched on to his, still a little dazed from her own orgasm. She reached up and cupped his face, a surprisingly gentle gesture in the midst of all this dirty fucking.

Somehow he knew it wasn't quite as simple as fucking. Not at this point, not anymore. His thrusts slowed and she held his face, watching him, moving with him, going from a frantic race to a slow dance. Moving together, sighing pleasure, their two bodies sliding against each other, more than just that release.

When the orgasm tightened his body, thrusting deep into her, she reached her arms around his neck and kissed him with a softness and a passion he didn't know could exist side by side.

But with Kayla, it somehow made all the sense in the world.

Chapter Fourteen

Kayla was pulled out of a very deep and warm sleep by the tinkling sound of her ringtone. She yawned, pawing at the nightstand next to her, trying to silence the sound before it woke up the very large man dead to the world next to her.

She smiled a little at that before realizing it was very dark and still very much night. She found her phone and hit answer in a panic. No one called late at night for a pleasant conversation. "Hello?"

"Kayla." The voice was breathless and faintly familiar, but not enough to put a name or face to it.

"Who is this?" she whispered.

"Aiden."

"Aiden?" She rubbed her eyes, trying to make sense of that. She pushed into a sitting position and Liam shifted next to her. "I . . . Is something wrong? Were you looking for Liam?"

"Liam? Why would I be looking for Liam by calling you?"

Kayla opened her mouth, but no sound or words came out. "I'm sorry. I don't understand . . ."

"Hey, I know I kind of disappeared there for a while, but I got everything sorted, and I just wanted to catch up on that rain check."

"Rain . . ."

"Who are you talking to?" Liam murmured sleepily.

"Who's that?" Aiden demanded, a sharp edge to his voice that was both just plain weird and a little creepy.

"Aiden, I don't know what possessed you to call me at . . ." She pulled the phone away from her face and looked at the time. "Two-thirty in the morning, but this is not okay."

"I'm sorry, Carrot. I just . . . Things have been so messed up the past few weeks. My head isn't on straight. Just let me—"

Out of nowhere the phone was being tugged out of her hands.

"Aiden, I don't know what the hell you think you're doing, but I'd end it pretty damn quick."

Kayla looked toward Liam's voice, but the room was too dark to see anything. But one thing was quite clear: Aiden had no clue that Liam had started something with her.

She felt oddly sick to her stomach at the revelation. It didn't matter, she supposed, but somehow her brain couldn't convince her body not to react.

"None of your damn business. What are you doing calling anyone in the middle of the night?" Liam demanded into her phone.

Kayla slipped out of bed and went to the bathroom. She flipped on the light, filling up the bedroom with a secondhand glow.

Liam's face was hard, his jaw tense, even his knuckles around her phone were white. "Fuck, don't. Aiden, listen to me. Aiden!" He swore roughly and threw back the covers, tossing her phone onto the bed as he grabbed his clothes and began tugging items on.

"What's going on?" Kayla asked, worry causing her heart to beat hard and some of her own hurt to die down. Maybe Aiden was in trouble and—

"He's getting fucking arrested, the moron." Liam jammed his feet into his socks, then zipped and buttoned his already pulled on pants.

"Liam . . . What are you going to do?"

"I'm going to go bail him out. Like my parents need his shit right now." He pulled on his shirt and started heading toward her bedroom door.

Part of her wanted to follow him and demand to know what he thought he was doing rushing out of here. But the stronger part of her kept her rooted in the spot by the bathroom door.

Coward. She closed her eyes against the little voice, but before she could work through her feelings on that she heard Liam retracing his steps.

She opened her eyes and he was standing before her, something like apology in his expression. "Sorry I have to run out like this," he said, leaning forward and brushing his mouth across hers. "But if I don't take care of it, he'll call Mom or, worse, Dad."

Kayla nodded like she understood. And she did understand. His dad was dealing with a heart problem, and his mother was understandably upset, and . . . for some reason the Patrick family seemed to need Liam to be the center. The fixer of all messes.

It seemed wildly unfair to her, but what did she know about functional, happy families? Zero.

"I'll make it up to you. I promise." He cupped her cheek with his rough hand, brushing his thumb over her cheekbone.

She tried to smile, but she failed. Hard. "You didn't tell him. About us."

Everything in him softened, even his shoulders slumped. "I haven't really seen him, Kayla."

"Except the other night when he said you didn't try to fix him," she returned, and even though she felt a little petty pointing it out, she couldn't stop herself. She felt . . . She didn't know. There was just this gut-twisting, heavy, sinking feeling in her stomach.

"He was drunk, Kayla. He passed out. It was hardly a conversation."

She should leave it at that, let him go, but all she could do was think of all the other ways he might have kept her a secret. "What about your parents?" she asked, looking at her bare feet.

"My parents?"

She could've kept being a coward and not said it, or not lifted her gaze, but this was part of everything about her new life. Having courage. Looking someone in the eye. Standing up. "Have you told them about us?"

His mouth just kind of dropped open as though taken completely off guard by her question. "Have you told yours?" he asked gently.

"I don't talk to mine," she replied, hugging her arms around herself because suddenly she felt cold and, well, alone. "Pretty much ever these days."

He scrubbed one hand over his jaw, but the other stayed on her face, holding on to her.

"I haven't. And I don't have any good excuses except things have . . . happened fast, but, listen, when everything settles down with my dad, we'll go over for dinner. Even invite Grandma." He searched her face for something, still rubbing that rough thumb slowly over her cheek. "Do you think I'm hiding you?"

"No. I . . ." She didn't know why she felt so hurt by all this. It had been a couple of nights, and while she felt a whole hell of a lot more, maybe he didn't, and he wouldn't be wrong.

But that didn't make her wrong either, did it? What would be wrong would be to shrink down and away, to shy away from hurt or embarrassment. That would be wrong. "It hasn't been very long at all, but I guess it feels . . ." Oh, if only words didn't desert her when she was nervous.

"Serious?"

His eyes seemed an impossible pale blue in the dim light, but they held her gaze as though—despite the fact his brother was getting arrested somewhere—she was the most important thing.

"Yes," she managed to whisper. "Serious. I-important."

He swallowed, but his other hand came up to cup her other cheek. "It is. To me. All of those things. I promise you."

She tried to breathe normally, but her chest was tight and her eyes were stinging. Serious. Important. Maybe something like love. It was almost too much.

"I have to go," he said gravely. "But call me when you wake up in the morning, okay?"

Kayla nodded wordlessly.

He pressed a kiss to her mouth, soft and sweet, something like a promise in and of itself. When he released her, she could see the regret in his eyes. So she forced herself to smile best she could. It wavered, surely, but it was better than nothing.

He turned and strode out of the room and Kayla simply stood there and waited until she heard her front door open, then close.

Then she sank to the end of her bed and let out a little sob. She didn't even know why she was crying, half hurt, half elation, so many *big* feelings fighting for space inside of her.

She took a deep breath and blew it out, trying to stem the tide of tears. Because this was good. All good. He felt the same way she did. *Serious and important.*

But she had the most obnoxious niggling worry in the back of her brain, that this kind of thing would always come between them. Problems would always need fixing, and he'd be the first to jump up to fix them.

"You like that about him," she reminded herself, aloud, in the quiet of her room alone. She forced herself to crawl back into bed and did her best to ignore that stupid, pointless worry.

* * *

Aiden hadn't ever been Mr. Rule Follower, but getting arrested for a DWI was not Aiden at all. Liam was just as much *worried* for his brother as he was pissed off at him for calling Kayla, for dragging him into this.

Liam drove to the police station frustrated and worried and wondering how on earth they would explain this to their parents, or if they even had to with everything else going on. Christ, his family was a damn mess.

Well, of course, things are going so well for you personally, this is what happens.

He shook that thought away and went into the police station. He was informed of what he needed to do, and went through all the steps, including paying the damn bond—money he was sure to never get back.

It took a little over an hour to go through all the rigmarole of getting Aiden out of jail. When they finally released him, Aiden only grinned. At Liam. At the other officers. He just grinned and grinned and grinned.

Liam didn't trust himself to say anything so he walked Aiden out to his truck in complete and utter silence. Once inside the truck, Liam looked at his brother. Okay, so he did have a few things to say. Well, one thing.

"So, what the fuck is wrong with you?"

"Aiden Patrick, nice to meet you."

Liam shook his head and started the truck, pulling out of the police department's parking lot. "This isn't you, Aiden."

Aiden laughed. "Like you know shit about who I am."

"I know you getting drunk every night is a problem. And I damn well know getting arrested is a big fucking problem, so why don't you stop feeling sorry for yourself and tell me what the fuck is wrong with you."

"You're fucking her. Fucking *my*—"

"She was never your anything, Aiden," Liam gritted out, hoping to end this line of conversation before his violent response bubbled over. Because Aiden had zero right to be pissed about him and Kayla. Zero. Right. "You disappeared, and—"

"You were what was left?"

It was a blow meant to hurt, and Aiden might be drunk and clearly in a shitty place in his life, but he knew how to land that blow right where it *would* hurt. "I'm not in the mood for your bullshit."

Aiden made a considering noise, and clearly the time in jail and the time it took to process everything had worn some of the drunk off of him. He was alarmingly with it, and happily mean.

These kinds of moods never ended well, and Liam was exhausted. By just about everything. But he took a deep breath and reminded himself that he had to be the bigger person when it came to Aiden.

Hadn't he been told his whole life he had to take the high road when his brother was being a manipulative ass? He was supposed to be the better person. The responsible, steady, counterpoint to Aiden's capricious, volatile immaturity.

Only Aiden had ever made Liam hate that role, but Liam had come too damn far to abandon it now. Mom and Dad had enough on their plates right now, and Liam *was* the better person, damn it.

So he ground his teeth together and drove to Mom and Dad's. He had a key and he could hopefully let Aiden in without waking anyone up, and then he could go home before he lost his tenuous grasp on control.

Liam pulled onto Mom and Dad's street, slowing down as he approached where he usually parked at the curb.

"What do you think would happen if she had the choice?" Aiden asked before Liam had come to a full stop.

Liam hit the brake hard, the screeching of his tires echoing through the quiet neighborhood. When he jammed the truck into park to stare at his brother, Aiden was only smiling. Mean and vicious.

Liam was pissed off, by and large, but he reminded himself that it was the middle of the night and surely, *surely* his brother was going through some huge crap to be being this much of an ass.

"If I, say, ran into her at the farmers' market, or maybe outside of her apartment, do you think she'd beg me off, or would she still agree to go out with me?"

"That'd be up to her, I guess," Liam forced himself to say through gritted teeth. He refused to let himself consider the question since it was wholly and utterly stupid and pointless. He pushed out of the truck, making sure his key to the front door was ready to go.

"She's sweet. Wouldn't want to hurt anyone," Aiden was saying as he got out of the truck and started following Liam—walking through the yard even though Dad had asked them approximately a million times to walk up the concrete drive in the spring so as not to disturb the grass seed or fertilizer he put down.

"But she always did have a thing for me. Probably be pretty hard to turn me down, especially if I was *persuasive*."

Liam whirled on his brother, shaking with a rage he was desperately, desperately trying to swallow down. "Say one more thing about her, Aiden," he said as calmly as he could manage, "one more damn thing and—"

"And you'll what? Perfect Saint Liam. What will you do to me, huh?" Aiden stepped closer, poking him in the chest. "Lecture me a little more *firmly*? Give me a real talking to if I wondered aloud how willing Kayla Gallagher would be to suck my—"

Liam threw the punch before he even thought about it, and the blow landed with a sickening crack and shot of pain down his arm.

Aiden stumbled to the ground, but before Liam had worked through the shock of actually punching his brother in the face, Aiden was back on his feet rushing him. Liam tried to brace himself, but Aiden's momentum knocked him flat on his back. Hard.

Aiden landed a solid punch to Liam's side and Liam's breath rushed out of his lungs. He managed to block Aiden's next punch, but he was in the crappier position here, underneath Aiden. He gave Aiden a push, but Aiden was using all his weight. So Liam elbowed Aiden in the stomach as hard as he could, using the blow to propel Aiden off of him. Aiden tried to get back up, and in the back of his mind, Liam thought maybe he should let him. Let him get up and say shit and whatever. Liam would take the high road like always.

Instead, he pushed his brother back down. "Get to your feet and I swear to God, I'll break something."

"And what would Mommy and Daddy think?" Aiden asked, the streetlight showing off the fact that something during the fight had split his lip, a thin trickle of blood down his chin. "I don't think Mom's going to be too happy with you."

"Fine. You want more of a fight? Fucking fine. Get it out of your system, Aiden. Stand up and we'll fucking fight."

Aiden got to his feet, fists balled in a fighter's stance. Liam rolled his eyes. "Oh, so we're going to box?"

"No, I'm going to break your fucking nose. I told you Kayla Gallagher was mine."

"Kayla is her own damn person. And a damned good one, and you were right the other day, you aren't good enough for her. Not by a fucking long shot. You're a spoiled baby masquerading as a fucking adult."

Aiden swung and Liam dodged it, but didn't realize Aiden had swung with the other arm as well. The blow hit him in the ear and made it ring, but Liam countered with one of his own, punching Aiden square in the gut.

Aiden doubled over and Liam took a step back. This was stupid and childish and—

Aiden kicked him right in the fucking shin. Liam howled in pain, before it turned into a growl of anger. This time he lunged at Aiden, tackling him back to the ground.

A light much closer than the street lamp flicked on, making them both wince.

"What on earth is going on here?" Mom demanded, her voice high and panicked. "Liam Patrick, get off your brother this instant!"

Shame washed through him, along with a bone-deep weariness. He didn't know what to do with Aiden. Never had. He didn't know how to see this as anything but inevitable, really. No, he'd never tried to fix Aiden because he damn well didn't know how.

And this was what it came down to. Liam couldn't wish it away, because he couldn't think of any alternatives to this right here. But he did wish they could have had better timing, that everything with Dad's stents was settled.

Liam got off Aiden and stood. He opened his mouth to try and find words that could ease Mom's worry or hurt, but there were none. None.

He couldn't help Aiden, because Aiden didn't want to help himself. And there was not a damn thing he could do about it. Liam couldn't help but wonder if that had caused the fight as much as anything else.

Mom rushed over and bent to help Aiden up to his feet, and Aiden let her. They both glared at him accusingly.

"Take me inside, Mom. I can't stand to look at him another minute," Aiden said, the rough, shaken note to his voice almost believable.

Mom cooed soothing words at Aiden, leading him inside, and Liam stood in the middle of the yard, breathing heavily, trying to make sense of any damn thing.

The door closed, sharp and final. Liam could only stare. He was pretty sure his nose was bleeding, and God knew his leg was throbbing from where Aiden had kicked him. He was out of breath and hurting inside and out.

And Mom had taken Aiden inside and shut the door on him.

Chapter Fifteen

Kayla hadn't slept much after Liam had left. She was too worried, and sort of vaguely irritated in a way she couldn't work through. She wasn't mad at Liam for leaving. He'd done the right thing. So maybe she was mad at Aiden. Or at a family who had somehow decided Liam had to solve all their problems.

Which wasn't fair. She didn't know much about his family, even if she knew Liam himself.

Fair or not, right or not, it was a simmering irritation in the back of her head as she drove from the donut place where she'd picked up some breakfast to Liam's house.

He'd said to call, but she didn't want to talk to him on the phone. She wanted to talk to him face to face and hear what had happened.

Maybe it was needy or insecure, but she needed some reassurance that this wasn't . . . Well, this *also* probably wasn't fair, but she was over worrying about fair for everyone but herself. This whole bravery thing meant not just saying what she wanted or going after it, but working toward it.

She pulled up in front of Liam's house. It was six thirty and his truck was parked at the curb, so he should be home. He might be sleeping, considering he'd left her place in the middle of the night, but if she knew Liam, he was probably awake and getting ready for work.

No matter how few hours he'd slept, no matter how much he'd helped his brother, he would consider it necessary to get up and work and make sure his dad didn't worry.

It was such an odd thing to be so impressed by that, but also a little irritated by it. Didn't he ever think to take care of himself?

Well, maybe that would just be her job. No one had ever let her take care of them before, and she liked taking care of Liam. It made her feel good.

She marched up to the front door, box of donuts in hand, and knocked firmly.

She waited. And waited. And waited. Maybe he was asleep. Or in the shower. Or maybe he'd gotten a ride from his father or something.

She should have called. This was stupid, inserting herself where she didn't belong.

Then the door opened and she exhaled.

"Hey." His voice was weird, more like a rasped whisper, and he had a baseball cap pulled low on his head, which was shading most of his face.

"Hi, I brought donuts. I thought you could use a sugary breakfast after last night."

His mouth curved, and that's when she noticed how puffy his lower lip looked, and the cut that definitely had not been there a few hours ago. "What happened to your lip?"

"Oh, that." He lifted a finger to his mouth, then angled his head down so the hat shielded her view of him almost completely.

She shied away from jumping to her own conclusions. Surely it was something innocuous. But he didn't explain either, or move to let her in.

Maybe a better person would have turned around and gone, but she didn't want to be a better person right this second. She reached up and yanked the hat off his head, and maybe it was overdramatic, but she gasped.

His cheek was visibly bruised and looked swollen. She reached out to touch his face, under the mark. "Liam."

"It's nothing. Really. A split lip. A bruise. I've had worse."

"How did it happen?" she demanded, and he finally met her gaze, everything about him looking exhausted and just . . . beaten.

"It's not important."

Rage propelled her forward. She nudged him out of the way so she could step inside. She dropped the box of donuts on an end table and marched into the kitchen.

"Not important," she muttered angrily as she wrenched open his freezer. He'd been hurt. *Hurt*. This man she lo— Well, she wasn't letting herself think like that quite yet, but Liam was important to her and it was physically painful that he'd been hurt and was saying it wasn't important.

She rummaged around until she found a frozen bag of vegetables. That would work. Then she marched back out to the living room where he was slowly closing the door. She pointed at his recliner.

"Sit."

"Kay—"

"Sit."

He huffed out a breath but crossed to the chair and sank into it. "I have to get to work," he grumbled irritably.

"You should have put ice on this," she replied, as if he hadn't spoken at all. She studied his bruise then. As carefully and slowly as she could, she pressed the bag to his cheek. He winced a little bit, but she slid into his lap, holding the bag of frozen carrots to his cheek.

He looked at her with that baffled expression she was learning to recognize even if she didn't always know where it came from.

"Now," she said, mustering all her firm determination, "tell me what happened."

He shifted a little underneath her, his arm coming around her waist and resting there. He didn't move his head from the bag, but his gaze slid away from hers. "It's not—"

"If you say it's not important, I will not be held responsible for my actions, Liam Patrick."

He sighed. "Aiden and I got into it a little bit. I shouldn't have . . ." He shifted again, but he held on to her as if to keep her in his lap. "He was pushing my buttons, and I lashed out. I know better."

"So you and Aiden got in an actual *fight*?"

"Um . . . Yes. It was a crappy mistake, Kay. I shouldn't have let him get to me that way. I threw the first punch. It was my mistake."

She gently touched his lip where it was puffy and split. "You both threw punches."

"Well, yes, but it never should have happened. I should have kept my cool. I knew what he was trying to do, and he succeeded. Mom heard us and came out and took Aiden inside and . . . Well, anyway. It's over. I won't be falling into that trap again, let me tell you."

"What did your mom do after she took Aiden inside?" Kayla asked, her stomach sinking sickly at what she suspected. But surely . . .

Liam shrugged ineffectively. "They went inside."

"What about you?"

"I went home."

"But . . . Walk me through this. I don't understand. You both fought? Because you hit him and he hit you?"

"Yes."

"But when your mom came outside, she only took Aiden in?"

"He was the one on the ground."

"Was he hurt worse than you?"

"I . . . I don't know. It doesn't matter. I have a house to go back to and—"

"And she ushered one of her children inside and did what with you? Ask if you were okay? Offer you some ice? Anything?"

"She . . . shut the door."

"Liam! That is . . . That is cruel. And unacceptable."

"Aiden—"

"I don't give a shit about Aiden. Her sons, both of them *her* sons, got in a fight and she chose one to take care of? Well, that is bullshit, Liam. Bull. Shit. How dare she?"

"He needs—"

"What about what you need, for heaven's sake?" She cupped the side of his face she wasn't holding the quickly thawing bag of carrots to. "What about you?"

He blinked at her as if she spoke some foreign language. Did he not . . . Did he *never* think about himself when it came to his family? It filled her with anger on his behalf and unease at what she was doing here, but she focused on the anger because this was utter crap.

She'd always assumed because Liam and his family had a relationship, they had to be a better, more loving family than the Gallaghers. Now she wasn't so sure.

"Kayla." He let out a breath, still looking at her in that baffled way, something like shock and reverence mixed in too. "I love you."

Kayla was sure her heart stopped. She knew her breathing had. He'd said . . . love, and not in any flippant, teasing sort of way. No, he was grave, so grave, and looking her right in the eye. She couldn't seem to breathe or move or respond.

Love. *Love.*

"What?" she breathed, stupidly.

"I know it's a little . . . soon, and I don't expect you to be there yet, but I'm not exactly a wishy-washy guy. I could probably talk myself out of it for a little bit longer, but what would be the point? I love you, Kayla. No one in my life has ever tried to take care of me, and even if someone's tried, I never would have let them, but when it's you? Hell, it's everything I want."

"Liam." Her throat was all closed up and she couldn't seem to get it to work to tell him all she was feeling.

"It's a lot and it's quick. Take some time—"

"I love you, too," she interrupted, trying to blink back the tears in her eyes.

He opened his mouth and she knew, just knew, he was going to say something about letting her take time or whatever other crap excuses, so she kept talking. "Don't you dare try to argue with me. I know what I feel, and it is love. I've never . . . No one has ever made me feel comfortable enough to be myself."

"You decided to do that. That doesn't have anything to do with me."

"It has *some* to do with you. Yes, I made a decision to change, but . . . Sometimes people come into your life who help you go down that path you need to go down, or give you a little nudge when you're learning a lesson that needs to be learned. Part of this change in my life is you, and I'm *glad*."

She laid the thawing bag of carrots down, rubbing her cold, damp hand up and down his leg to warm it up before she used it to cup his face. To look into those beautiful blue eyes and brush a light kiss over his poor swollen mouth.

"I love you," she said, with all of the courage that she'd decided to have, and all the courage Liam had given her.

He leaned forward, kissing a tear that had trailed halfway down her cheek. And then he pulled her so that she was leaning against him, curled against his shoulder, still sitting in his lap.

She wasn't sure how long they sat like that, basking in this big, complex emotion between them, but Kayla knew it was a memory she'd always cherish.

A week passed and Liam didn't try to go home. He saw his dad at work, and Dad didn't mention anything about Aiden. Liam figured he was too focused on the stent surgery to worry about his sons being dipshits.

Every night, he either spent with Kayla at her place, or she was at his. She'd taken a short temp job while she waited to hear back about her job interview at the orchard, and since her hours were shorter than his, she usually made him dinner or breakfast.

She painted Dinah's birthday present, and they went together to Dinah's birthday dinner. Kayla came with him for the Gallagher & Ivy Farmers' Market and charmed people into buying all manner of things.

It ate at him that he didn't know what was going on with Mom or Aiden, but Kayla was always telling him it was for the best. If he went over and checked on them, he'd get sucked into something that wasn't his business.

She was right. He tried to tell himself she was right. He tried to focus on being in love with someone, on that someone not just taking care of him, but clearly enjoying it. He tried to focus on building a *foundation* with this amazing woman who so often put him first.

It was like another world, and it was nowhere near comfortable. But for Kayla? He'd drown in discomfort.

Still, he was glad he had a little extra to work on with Patrick & Son Patch-ups, even if he hated Dad's upcoming stent surgery being the reason. It was good to be in his own head and make sure he thought he was on the right path.

Kayla waiting for him convinced him it was every time.

Liam loaded up his truck and hated the way a day without Dad reminded him of those months after the heart attack. The fear and the nerves. The loneliness of carrying all this on his back and the pressure of making sure he did as good of a job.

And yet the thing that was different this time, aside from the preworry, was that he could go to Kayla's tonight and she'd talk to him and make him feel better. She couldn't make him forget, but she *eased* things a little bit, like magic.

But maybe that was just love and shit.

Buoyed by the prospect of a meal with Kayla, Liam was smiling as he started his truck. His phone chimed and he pulled it out of his pocket, glancing at the text.

Mom: *Please come over.*

He stared at the text for the longest time. He knew Kayla wouldn't approve, and maybe she was right. Maybe he needed to make himself less available to his family so they understood he wasn't the fix to everything.

But there was this . . . *thing* inside of him. Something like a compulsion. How did you just not help your family?

He responded to Mom, then brought up a text to Kayla. He winced a little as he wrote the lie. *Working a little late. Will call when I'm on my way.*

He'd tell her the truth when he got to her place. It would be better to tell her in person, and who knew what it was about? Maybe Mom just wanted to see him.

You could have asked why she did.

He ignored the voice in his head and drove toward his parents' house. Dad's surgery was tomorrow. Maybe Mom wanted everyone together even though Dad had all but forbidden any family gathering.

Dad wanted to dwell in his worry and fear alone, and Liam couldn't blame him for that, but this was hard on Mom, too. It was hard and scary for all of them.

He parked in front of his parents' house, steeling himself to be strong. Strong enough not to fall into any Aiden traps of getting pissed, and strong enough to avoid manipulation. If he could help make Mom feel better, he would. If he couldn't, well, he'd have to live with that too.

Mom came out of the house, closing the door behind her. She looked pale and worn and he knew this surgery was weighing heavily on her. Mostly, Liam surmised, because Dad was threatening to give up if it didn't work.

There was nothing wrong with being here or comforting her. There was nothing wrong about giving to his family. Kayla would understand that in the wake of everything that was going on.

"Hey, Mom. Everything okay?"

She shook her head, hugging her arms around herself. "No." She sniffled. Clearly she'd already been crying, though she wasn't at the moment. "I'm worried, Liam. I'm so worried."

"I know, Mom. But we have to try to be positive and just hang in there." He pulled his mother into a hug, hoping to infuse some physical strength into her. "Worrying about what might happen after isn't going to do us any good."

Mom's brows drew together as she pulled away from him. "After what?"

"After the surgery."

"I wasn't . . . I'm not talking about your father. I mean, I'm worried, don't get me wrong, but we've done this before and he has an excellent doctor. I'll be a mess tomorrow, but Aiden is who I'm sick over right now."

Liam could not believe his ears. Couldn't begin to comprehend . . . "What?"

"Liam, this week has been awful. Just awful. I think he's been doing drugs. And I'm worried he might hurt himself. He's so depressed. So low."

Liam stepped away completely, though part of him still wanted to hug her, still wanted to offer help. There was still this part of him certain that if he helped enough . . . He didn't let himself finish that thought. "Maybe he needs professional help."

"I tried to suggest it, but . . ." She looked away, biting her lip as she wrung her hands together. "Listen, I think if we can get him to a better place, we can convince him to see a therapist, but right now? He's so worked up about this Kayla Gallagher thing."

Liam did his best to stomp out his temper before it started to bubble. "There is no Kayla Gallagher *thing*."

"Well, Aiden did have his eye on her fir—"

"I have to go." He had to stand up for himself when it came to this. He wouldn't be manipulated into thinking he'd done something wrong or that he'd somehow *stolen* something. He and Kayla *loved* each other.

"No, please, baby." Mom grabbed his hand, and he could have easily tugged out of her grip, but that seemed wrong. She was upset. Maybe it wasn't right or fair that she was more worried about Aiden than anyone else, but Aiden was still her kid. Even if Liam was too.

"I know this isn't fair. I know it. But can't you just break up with that girl? Even for a little while? I know Aiden isn't thinking straight, but he's just certain you've stolen her from him. I know that's not how women or the world work, but . . . I'm so afraid, Liam."

"You want me to break up with Kayla because Aiden thinks . . . I'm sorry, how does that help?"

"He's just so down. You don't understand. I've never seen him like this. He thinks you have everything, and he's worthless." A sob escaped Mom's lips. "I can't lose all of you. What if he hurts himself, and something happens to your father, and you aren't talking to me?"

"Mom."

"Please." She grabbed his hands, tears streaming down her face.

"Please, I'll never ask anything of you again. I'm so scared for him. Just . . . Just break things off with her for a bit. Until we can convince Aiden to get some help."

"And if we never convince him?"

Mom started sobbing in earnest. "Don't say that, Liam. Don't say it can't be fixed."

It broke him, piece by piece, to see his mother openly cry. She was always emotional about movies or books or causes, but she rarely got overly emotional about real things. She kept that in check, and Dad did too, and it was hard to watch her be so *broken* by something he could fix.

By breaking up with Kayla.

It was ludicrous. Ridiculous. The exact kind of thing Kayla was talking about when she said his family had unreasonable expectations of him.

But his mother was sobbing, begging, and . . . What would Liam do if Aiden *did* hurt himself? Even if he wasn't at fault? Even if this really had nothing to do with Kayla, how did he . . . How did he let his brother self-destruct?

"I don't . . . I don't know what to say to you right now," Liam forced out, his voice a pained whisper into a beautiful spring evening.

"Could you just tell me you'll consider it? Please?" She squeezed his hands in hers, looking up at him with hope and desperation in her gaze, and Liam didn't know how to say no. Not to her. Not to himself. "I can't stand the thought of him hurting himself, Liam. I can't stand it. I've tried so hard to love him, to give him everything, and no matter what I do . . . Where did I go so wrong with him, when you're so good?"

Liam reversed their hands so he was holding hers now. He gave a squeeze. "I'll see what I can do, all right?"

Mom's entire face brightened, and she let out another squeaky sob before flinging her arms around him. "Oh, Liam. Thank you. Thank you. I know you can fix this. I know it."

He wasn't sure how long those words would haunt him, but he knew they would.

Chapter Sixteen

Liam was quiet, and Kayla couldn't get over the inclination that something was wrong, no matter how much he protested that it wasn't.

He wasn't exactly an effusive guy, but he was always relaxed with her. In a way she'd begun to notice was special. Even when he smiled and talked happily with a customer at the farmers' market, he didn't . . .

She didn't know the word for it exactly. It was just, she understood why she'd always seen him as sort of hard and standoffish before she'd gotten to know him. There was a kind of wall he kept up between himself and people even when he was helping them.

But he didn't have that with her. Or he hadn't lately, but tonight, it was definitely there. It bothered her and it worried her, but she also didn't want to nag him constantly. Maybe he needed some space to worry about his father's surgery alone. She just wished he'd *tell* her that.

She could ask him, and maybe she would, but . . . she wanted it to come from him. She wanted him to take that step to laying his problems at her feet without her having to pull them out of him.

Would that ever happen?

With that depressing thought making her gut twist, she cleared the table, taking the dishes to the kitchen sink. She took a deep breath and tried to get her head on straight. Liam had a lot on his mind with his father's surgery tomorrow. She had to cut him some slack.

This new leaf wasn't just about barging through life and getting whatever she wanted because she'd once hid in the corners and not gone after anything. It was about balance. *Love* was about balance.

"I hope you know how much I appreciate this," Liam said, coming up behind her, wrapping his arms around her waist.

It was amazing that something as simple as a hug and appreciation could wipe all that worry and confusion away. She smiled over her shoulder at him. "I know."

"And how do you know that?" he asked, leaning forward enough to rest his chin on her shoulder.

She turned in the circle of his arms, wrapping hers around his neck. "You've shown your appreciation in a great many creative ways." She rubbed one hand across his beard and some of that ache was back. She'd spent an entire dinner pretending there wasn't this heavy weight on his shoulders, and she didn't think she could move on to sex knowing it was there. If he begged her off, she'd let him, but maybe what Liam really needed was someone to ask. "What's bothering you?"

He blew out a breath. "Can't get anything by you."

"I hope that always continues. Now, tell me."

"So bossy." But his smile quickly died. "I, um, went to . . . visit my mom."

Kayla did her best not to react unfavorably. Based on what she'd gleaned from Liam, and knowing Mr. Patrick even if only as Gallagher's handyman, she had a theory that Liam's mother was the center of a lot of his . . . hangups. But Mr. Patrick *was* having surgery tomorrow, and Kayla should be kind. "Is she upset about tomorrow?"

"I thought so. I mean, she is. But she's, um, worried about Aiden."

Kayla didn't want to butt in about family stuff. She really didn't. When it came to Liam misguidedly putting himself last, well, she'd said a few things, but when it came to actual relationships, she didn't want to start nosing into things that didn't really have anything to do with her.

But it was hard to bite her tongue. It irked her on every level that there seemed to be an odd kind of favoritism toward Aiden, and though she didn't have any siblings, she knew what it was like to be overlooked.

Grandmother had always focused everything on Dinah, and Kayla had tried to contort herself into a million little obedient pieces to get noticed, to feel loved. It had never happened.

Liam didn't do the same thing, but it was for the same reasons, but he didn't see it. Was it her job to help him see it? Could it be?

"She thinks Aiden is maybe getting into drugs now. She's afraid he's going to hurt himself."

"It sounds like he needs professional help," Kayla returned as blandly as she could manage.

"He does, and I suggested it, but . . . Aiden's not particularly apt to take a suggestion. Mom thinks . . . Well, she thinks if we can get him a little more even-keeled he'd listen. She asked for my help."

This time Kayla really did bite her tongue and she stepped away, no matter how much she knew he'd read into that. Aiden's issues were so completely not her place, but she didn't like how everyone seemed to insist Liam could fix Aiden if only Liam tried.

"I know you feel responsible for Aiden, for your family, and I understand that," she said as carefully as she could. "But you are not a mental health professional, Liam, and if Aiden really is that bad off, that's what he needs."

"I know. I know. But, see, he's got this idea in his head that he's unhappy because . . ."

Liam looked meaningfully at her and Kayla couldn't help it. She rolled her eyes. "Because of *me*?"

"Well, us."

She laughed. Meanly. She shouldn't have, she knew it, but this was so utterly ridiculous. "So you have something he doesn't, and he does drugs and hurts himself? I don't think so, Liam. That sounds like a very convenient excuse."

"Maybe it is, Kay. I get that. It's not like I don't get that he's fixated on something that has nothing to do with him for all the wrong reasons, but he's going to keep being that way until we can get him some help."

Liam looked so *sad,* and it poked at her that she wasn't being more sympathetic. He wanted to help the people he loved, and was that really so awful? "What can I do?"

He took a deep breath, because clearly Liam had some plan and he wanted her help, and maybe if she helped . . . Well, she had nothing against Aiden. She didn't think he was a very good brother, but maybe he did need help, and if she could do that . . . Well, it would make Liam happy, and wasn't that what she really wanted?

"If Aiden thinks we're not together, it might calm him down enough for us to convince him to seek some professional help. Just for a little while. We'd stay apart, but we can still talk. It'd just be like . . . a long-distance relationship. For a little while. Until we can convince him to get some help."

It was a blow. Kayla had always known words could hurt, could knock you back a few paces, but this . . . She had to blink at the sudden stinging in her eyes, swallow at the nauseating roll of her stomach. "You want to pretend like we broke up, and basically *act* like we broke up. Actually be apart." She didn't bother to keep the hurt out of her voice. This *hurt*.

"Just for a little bit." He stepped toward her but she moved away and shook her head and he stopped.

"How long?" she demanded.

"What? I don't . . ."

"A week? A month? A year?"

"It wouldn't be a year."

She shook her head, hugging herself tighter. "But maybe a few months?"

"I can't predict . . . I know it seems harsh, but if he's really threatening to hurt himself . . . My dad is having surgery tomorrow. And if it doesn't work . . . My family is barely holding on right now, okay? I need to do what I can."

"You really believe that, don't you?"

He blinked, whether surprised by the sharpness of her tone or surprised he didn't have a good answer for that, she didn't know. Maybe she didn't care.

"Of course I believe that," he said, his voice rough and baffled. "Look, maybe you don't understand because you don't have a close-knit family, but—"

"Close-knit my ass, Liam. You have a family who treats you like dirt, and news flash, no amount of fixing things is going to change that." It was harsh, and too much, but she was just so angry and hurt and . . .

How could he think this was okay? How could he think it was his duty to fix a jackass who blamed his own brother's happiness for his problems?

She'd spent her life reining in her temper and trying to keep people from seeing her hurt, but she was done with that. She wasn't going to be the sacrifice Liam made for his family, even if that meant she had to walk away.

* * *

Liam was frozen. Kayla's words hurt, but in a way he couldn't have predicted. Like some kind of truth cutting its way down to his very soul.

Except it was bullshit. Of course his family cared, and they didn't treat him like dirt. She was witnessing an extreme case, but it hadn't always been like this, and it wouldn't always be.

If they got Aiden help things would be different. He had to believe that. "I'm not explaining this right, clearly."

"Or you could consider the possibility that you're just wrong."

She was standing there, her eyes shiny with tears, and he knew she didn't understand, because if she understood, she wouldn't be hurt like this. And that was on him, her hurt. He'd messed this up, but he could fix it. He just had to find the right combination of words and he could fix it.

"Okay, how about this?" She swallowed, still hugging herself so tight. He should be the one hugging her. But she wouldn't let him. "Take a second to imagine years down the road. Let's say we got married. Maybe even had kids."

Every word she said felt like a dagger. This even more so than what had come before because it was all too easy to picture. A future with Kayla. A family of his own. Something he'd never spent much time thinking about.

He didn't think about the future. There always seemed to be so many problems in the here and now to fix, he never thought about what might come next.

"Then let's say, suddenly Aiden decides your life is better and he's going to harm himself because of it. I'm supposed to believe you'd stick around *that* time when you're not sticking around *this* time?"

"Don't insult me like that. I would never . . ." Why was she talking about a future when they had to get through the present first?

"But now is different because . . . Why, exactly? You said you loved me. So why should I think anything would change? He'll always come first."

"There's no hierarchy, Kay. You don't seem to understand how grave this situation is."

"No, Liam. I do. I don't expect it to be easy, and I know life isn't fair. But I know, I *know*, at some point you have to choose. Because you can't keep fixing everyone. Especially when they very purposefully don't want you to fix them. He wants to punish you. He wants to manipulate you, because he *can*."

"He's my brother." It was the only thing Liam could think to say. How did you walk away from helping your own family? It wasn't like he was suggesting they actually break up. He wasn't choosing Aiden over her. He was just . . . rearranging things until they could maneuver Aiden into some help.

Was that really so much to ask?

"He's his own fucked-up person," Kayla replied, and a tear slipped over her cheek, practically killing him where he stood. "You can't make him not that, and trust me—because been there, done that—your mom won't magically love you more if you do what she wants."

She kept saying shit like that and he didn't know how to argue with it. But he had to find a way because she was wrong. She didn't see it the way he did. How could she?

"This isn't some warped crusade to get my mother's love or approval. I have that. I'm sorry you don't, but we're not the same."

She laughed, that same nasty laugh from earlier. Nothing sweet or soothing as her laugh normally was.

"Okay, we're not the same. Then I guess you've never done something in the hopes it would get noticed or earn you a pat on the back or a good job. You've never gotten so used to doing what they want you to do, you don't even know what *you* want to do."

"I know what I want to do," he ground out.

"Fix everything?"

She said it so condescendingly, and it grated. He'd never been anything but honest and straightforward with her. He'd never hidden those fixer impulses. He wasn't suddenly showing his true colors. He'd been this all along.

"This isn't exactly what I expected from my girlfriend the night before my father's surgery."

"Well, it's not really what I expected either since we aren't talking about your father. We're talking about your brother."

"It all connects, Kayla. It's my family."

She inhaled deeply, and some of that harshness on her face left, but he didn't like what was left any better. It was all soft hurt and more tears.

"I get it. I do. You don't want to think we're alike, but I understand this, Liam. You don't want to admit what they're doing to you because it feels good to help. You feel valuable." She stepped forward and touched him for the first time since this conversation had gone horribly wrong. She looked up at him imploringly. "I value you, and I don't expect you to fix me in return. I love you, and that means I want *you* to be happy—it makes me happy. Yeah, maybe Aiden needs some help. Maybe he's not in the best place, but if you *losing* is the only thing that makes him even receptive to getting help, that isn't love and it isn't family, not one worth sacrificing for."

"I think that's easy for you to say." He didn't know why those words came out. He knew she was trying to help. He knew she didn't mean her words to cause this river of pain to flow through him. But everything she said felt too close to right.

But if she was right, who the hell was he? What kind of life was he living. She just didn't understand.

Her hand dropped from his chest and she stepped away, crossing her arms over her chest. Her expression was hard again, furious. And that poked at his own fury he was desperately trying to leash.

"Easy, huh?"

"Yeah, I think it's pretty damn easy to judge my family's treatment of me when you just ran away from yours instead of standing up to them or trying to understand them. Maybe I should be worried about future Kayla. Maybe when you're unhappy, when you're feeling like you're decoration, of your own damn doing, you'll run away."

She inhaled sharply and there was a moment of clear, unfiltered pain on her face. She didn't even bother to hide it. She didn't look away. She didn't straighten her shoulders. She stared right at him looking wrecked.

"Well, I'm glad I see what you really think of me."

"We're both angry and saying things we don't—"

"I meant every word I said, so don't bother to try and fix this too, Liam. You made your choice, and it's time for me to make mine. I'd like you to leave."

He took a step toward her, apologies on his lips. He didn't want to leave. This had gotten completely out of hand, and if she let him . . . If she gave him some time he could make sense of this. He *could* fix this.

"Now," she said firmly, stalking toward the door. "I have nothing left to say to you." She wrenched it open and pointed.

He took a deep breath, trying to calm the panic beating through him. The panic wouldn't help. He needed to be calm and rational and he'd work this out. "I'll go because you've told me to, but I don't consider this over."

She lifted her chin and looked him right in the eye as he stepped into the hallway. "Well, I do. And congratulations. Aiden got exactly what he wanted." She slammed the door in his face before he could respond to that.

Not that he could. He had no words. He didn't understand any of this. All he felt was numb.

And very, very alone.

Chapter Seventeen

Kayla sat in Dinah and Carter's kitchen and stared at the cupcake Dinah had shoved in front of her. She'd spent most of last night crying, and then she'd spent her morning finishing up her temp job and worrying about Liam and his father.

She *hated* that she was worried about the jerk, but she was. Couldn't help it. If anything went wrong in that surgery, Liam would somehow find a way to blame himself. And that was stupid and obnoxious and he should know better.

But she wanted to be the one to teach him, even when she was so damn mad at him she'd imagined herself punching him in the balls more than once.

"Eat it," Dinah demanded, swiveling the plate with the cupcake back and forth. "It'll do a broken heart good."

"Aren't you supposed to go back to work? Grandmother will not be happy with you taking an extra-long lunch break."

"Grandmother can bite me."

Kayla looked dolefully at her cousin.

"Okay, Grandmother can maybe not bite me, but she will deal. I have plenty of personal time to take. You need a cupcake and a shoulder to cry on."

"I need a boyfriend who isn't an asshole."

"Oh, those don't exist," Dinah replied decidedly, sticking her finger in the frosting on the cupcake and taking a little bite to her mouth.

"You love Carter," Kayla pointed out, taking her own little finger scoop of frosting.

"Yes, I do. Immeasurably. I'd do anything for him, and sometimes I love him so much it physically hurts. And sometimes he's an asshole and I want to punch him in the junk." Dinah shrugged. "Likely, he feels the same about me. I've come to the conclusion that that's just love."

Kayla couldn't manage a smile, though she knew she should try. "I'm really not hungry, Dinah."

"But it's chocolate."

Kayla did manage a smile at that. "You don't think I should apologize? Maybe . . . Maybe I overreacted. His dad is having surgery today. I was too hard on him."

"Do you really think that?"

Kayla heaved out a breath and rested her chin on her arms. "No."

"Then there's your answer."

"But if I'm right, why am I miserable?"

"Oh, honey." Dinah reached across the table and squeezed her arm. "I don't know that anything in life that's *right* is ever easy. Especially when you add in love and other people. It's kind of a recipe for misery."

"That's—" Her phone rang and she nearly jumped. She scrambled for it, and she'd be embarrassed by doing so in front of Dinah later.

But it wasn't Liam. It was the phone call she'd been waiting for from the orchard she'd interviewed at, and she should be excited rather than disappointed.

Still, when she answered she couldn't seem to muster nerves or excitement or anything other than an Eeyore depression. "Hello?"

"Good morning, is this Ms. Gallagher?"

"Yes."

"Wonderful. This is Sheila from Tiffer's Farm & Orchard. I'm going to be kind of blunt because I know how stressful it is waiting for an answer on a job. Unfortunately we decided to go another way with the position you applied for."

"Oh." It was disappointing. If she hadn't spent all night crying over Liam, she might have even cried, but all she managed to feel was kind of numb.

"But we did want to offer you an alternate position."

"Alternate . . . position?"

"We really liked you a lot for the position, but another applicant had way more experience. However, we have three locations and if you'd be interested and willing, there is a lower-level position at our New Benton location. It'd give you the kind of experience we'd be looking for the next time a position opened up."

"O-oh." Kayla took a deep breath and willed herself to focus. This was her life. Her real life, and yes it sucked that Liam wasn't going to be a part of it, but that didn't change the reality of her future. It was still going to be there. She still had to build it.

"Let me tell you a little bit about the responsibilities, and then if you need some time to decide, we can give you a few days."

So Kayla listened to the description of the job. It did feel a little bit like a demotion from her position at Gallagher's, but it would also be a position she got all on her own. The location was farther away than the one she'd applied at, but she could move.

She could do anything. It was her life to build. Part of her wanted to decline and to go home and hide in her bed. Pine over Liam. Pine over leaving Gallagher's.

But she had changed these past few months, and when she and Liam had told each other their I-love-yous, she'd said that he'd been a part of her change. She'd needed him to make that next step, and even if she didn't have him for this next, next step, it would be stupid to regress just because he wasn't here.

He certainly wouldn't go cry in his house every night because things hadn't gone according to plan. No, he was somewhere out there determined to fix everything.

"If you need time to consider—"

"No, I'd love to take the job. It sounds perfect."

"Wonderful. I'm going to pass all your contact information to Jess over at the New Benton location, and she will get in touch about start dates and training, if that sounds good."

"Yes, thank you. Really. I'm very excited to start."

"Welcome to Tiffer's, Ms. Gallagher. I think you'll be an excellent addition to our team."

"Th-thank you. Goodbye."

Kayla clicked and stared at her phone until Dinah grabbed her and gave her a little shake.

"You got the job!"

Kayla looked up at her cousin, who was grinning widely. "Well, not *the* job, but *a* job. A good start."

"That's awesome, Kay." Dinah didn't let go of her arm. Instead, she rubbed a palm up and down it, a reassuring gesture. "A good start is exactly what you need."

Kayla agreed. It was absolutely what she needed, but she couldn't seem to help it. She just burst into tears.

Liam sat in the waiting room at the hospital breathing slowly and carefully. He wanted to fidget and pace, but Mom was doing enough of that for both of them. And considering the way Grandma was glaring at her, Liam didn't think he needed to add to it.

Aiden was missing, and Liam knew that was half of Mom's worry. Liam was counting down the minutes before Mom asked him to go on a search.

Something that sounded far too much like Kayla's voice in his head whispered about how unfair that request would be.

Which was fucking stupid since Mom had asked nothing of him today. Why was he already trying to defend himself against it?

He leaned forward, elbows on his knees, raking his fingers through his hair, trying to just breathe. It was all he could do. He had no control over what was happening with Dad. No control over where Aiden was. He couldn't *do* anything.

He couldn't fix anything. And that made his throat close up so tight he couldn't breathe. Mom stopped pacing and took the seat next to him, sliding her hand across his back in a comforting gesture.

It helped his throat open up, helped him manage a breath. That's what family did. Reached out and comforted each other.

"You did it, right?"

The jolt of hurt hit fast and unexpected, like missing a nail head and smashing your finger with a hammer. You should have been paying more attention. You should have seen it coming.

But there you were, smashed, painful thumb throbbing and all you could do was accept this as your reality.

He clenched his jaw, too many feelings fighting for prominence so he simply nodded sharply. Yes, he had done exactly what Mom had asked, more thoroughly than she could even imagine.

Mom leaned her head on his shoulder, wrapping her hands around his arm and giving it a little squeeze. "Thank you," she whispered. "It's going to make a difference. I just know it."

And yet, Aiden wasn't here. Dad was in surgery. What difference was he making?

He was helping Mom. That mattered, and it wasn't some attempt to earn her affection. He had it. It was right here.

"Aiden!" Mom hopped up and ran over to where Aiden stepped into the waiting room. She flung her arms around him and simply stood there, saying something Liam couldn't hear.

Probably for the best.

"What did you do?"

Liam blinked over at his grandmother. "Huh?"

"The thing your mother asked you, what was it?"

He shrugged ineffectively. Grandma and Mom had always had a kind of tense relationship. Not antagonistic, but certainly not close. Definitely a lot of veiled disapproval from both. "It doesn't matter. Just a favor for Aiden."

Grandma rolled her eyes. "Oh, for heaven's sake."

Liam didn't say anything to that and he didn't try to read into it. He'd had his fill of people telling him what they thought of his favors. He looked down at his hands as his grandmother grumbled something about it not being her place.

Then she slapped him across the shoulder.

"What was that for?"

"For sitting there looking all wounded and ruining my Zen."

Christ. He couldn't catch a break. "I'm sorr—"

"Don't be sorry, Liam Connor Patrick. I told myself I'd stay out of it when your father asked me to, but I am done. My son is in surgery and I will darn well speak my mind. It isn't right, and you're all old enough to know better."

"Grandma," Liam said, forcing his voice to be even and soothing as he glanced to make sure Mom hadn't heard her slap or outburst. "I don't know what you're talking about, but we should just calm—"

"Your mother loves a cause. Aiden's always been her cause." Grandma jerked her chin in Mom and Aiden's direction. "Liam, you have always been the martyr for her cause. And none of you see it. Not one of you. Not even your father. He told me to stop butting my nose in where it didn't belong, so I did, but I'm fed up."

"I'm not a martyr."

"But you look miserable and you've done a favor for Aiden. Sacrificing yourself for him all over again and for what?"

"For my family."

Grandma made a rude noise. "Family doesn't force you into abject misery. *Family* stands with each other, not for one person. Family doesn't punch each other down so you're on the same level. You raise up who you can, and you pray for those you can't. A real family knows that love is as selfish as it is selfless."

"Grandma, that doesn't make any sense."

"It does to me," she replied, her mouth sinking at the corners, the wrinkles in her face seeming deeper and harsher today. But she pushed to her feet. "I'm going to go pray . . . or get a drink," she muttered before stalking out of the waiting room and into the hospital hallway.

Liam didn't know what to do with all of that. Unfortunately it felt all too much like Kayla's words last night. Too many truths that didn't make sense when compared to what he'd always believed.

But how could it be the truth if he didn't believe it? How could he be a martyr when he'd never given up anything for Aiden? Maybe a few days off when Aiden had worked for Dad. Sure, he'd paid Aiden's way quite a few times. And, yes, he'd given a good chunk of his savings to help pay for Aiden to go to culinary school a few years back.

But how was that not raising Aiden up because he could? He'd had the cash, and Mom and Dad and Aiden hadn't. At the time, Aiden had needed some training more than Liam had needed a new roof.

He wasn't punched down. He was a good fucking brother, damn it.

Mom came and sat beside him again and Liam scanned the room, frowning. "Where'd Aiden go?"

"He was going to go buy everyone some soda." Mom smiled and patted Liam's knee. "I told him about you and Kayla. He didn't say anything, but we'll work on him some more once your father's out of surgery."

He looked at his mother, so pleased with herself when they still didn't know how Dad's surgery had gone. He could see the worry lines on her face, and he knew that she did worry, and he almost wondered if she was fixating on Aiden because it was something she could control and Dad's health was something she couldn't.

Oh shit.

That wasn't what he was doing. He hadn't been fixated. He'd been happy with Kayla, and yes he had jumped at the chance to help . . .

Oh shit, shit, shit. He was a fucking martyr.

"What did your grandmother say to you?" Mom asked, trying to sound casual and failing.

Liam shook his head. "Nothing. Nothing new. Just the same question people have been asking me for years." And it was true. He'd never put the pattern together before, but neither Kayla nor Grandma asking him what he was doing was some brand-new revelation.

It was harder to brush off from people he loved so much. Friends? The occasional girlfriend? It had been easy to decide they just didn't get it—couldn't. But Grandma was a part of this family, and Kayla had so quickly become something like his heart.

"What question?" Mom asked gently. Because that was the hard part, the part that made it so hard to end. Mom meant well. She cared. It wasn't as though she didn't love him or magically loved Aiden more. It was just what Grandma had said. Aiden was the project, and Mom knew what to do with projects.

She knew less what to do with him, except recruit him in those projects, and he was powerless to that.

"Why I do it. Why I'm always trying to fix things."

"Because you're a good man, sweetie. Why would that even be a question?"

"Because I'm not happy, Mom. I'm in love with Kayla. I'm not happy being apart—pretend or real, though it's pretty damn real considering she didn't love our little idea."

"Oh, Liam. I'm sorry she didn't understand, but you're doing the right thing. We'll get Aiden the help he needs now. We can make him happy and secure. I'm sure of it."

Liam looked at his hands. Hands rough from work and giving it his all, and still . . . They'd always been here, trying to fix Aiden. No matter what it took. No matter what Liam had to give. No matter if Liam was happy or not. "Is his happiness more important than mine?" he managed to scratch out, almost afraid of the answer.

"Of course not! Honey . . . Aiden's just . . . He isn't as strong as you. He needs more help. If that woman didn't understand that, if she doesn't support you loving your brother, she isn't the girlfriend you want. I've never cared for the Gallaghers."

Liam could only stare at his mother as she most purposefully did not meet his shocked gaze. She stared at some bland-ass painting on the wall across from them.

Never cared for the Gallaghers. *That* woman. He had the sinking fear this was just as much about him as Aiden. As much about Mom keeping a hold on him as it was about helping Aiden get better.

His heart shied away from the thought, but it was all too plain to let his heart lead. There was too much heartbreak to let those soft parts of him lead.

"As soon as we know Dad's all right, I'm going to go see her. I'm not going to lie or pretend. Not for Aiden. Not for you."

"Not for your family?" Mom demanded, tears filling her eyes, her lip trembling as she studied him as though he were some stranger.

Maybe he was. Maybe he needed to be. "I have never been first in this family, and I don't even care about that. I work hard and I give as much as I can, but I'm not going to give what isn't fair. It isn't fair to me, and it isn't fair to Kayla."

"And what about Aiden?"

"Maybe Aiden needs to learn how to help himself."

"I don't know what your grandmother said to you, but she is wrong and you will regret turning your back on us, Liam Patrick. Shame on her. Shame on you." Mom said it with such vehemence, he wanted to relent. He wanted to soothe.

But it wouldn't ever end. That was the thing. He was thirty fucking years old and this only ever escalated. This only ever ended up with him giving up more and more.

He didn't want to give up Kayla. He never had, but seeing the situation more clearly made it even more disgusting what he'd asked of her. What he'd expected her to understand.

When she had never asked too much of him. When she had taken his burdens as her own. When she had comforted him. She had given, and she had taken, because apparently she knew how to be in a reciprocal relationship.

He didn't. Never had, but damn, it was so much better than this. It wasn't easy and it wasn't simple, but it gave so much more than it took.

"Liam—" Mom's voice was shrill and Liam fought for calm and control. For his heart, and for his courage. He was not a coward, but he'd been doing an excellent impression of one.

"I won't fight with you here," he said quietly and evenly as other people in the waiting room began to stare at them. "I won't fight with you now. But I hope when we get Dad home and back on his feet . . . I hope you'll think a little bit about what you've asked me to do for Aiden, and what you've ever asked Aiden to do for himself."

Mom stared at him as if he'd slapped her, but she said nothing else, and when they had the news that Dad had come through with flying colors, Liam knew exactly what came next.

Chapter Eighteen

"You didn't have to come home with me."

"Of course I did," Dinah said cheerfully. "Carter all but shoved me out the door."

Kayla eyed Dinah as they walked up the stairway to her apartment door. "Yeah, that was . . . weird."

But Dinah only grinned. "So weird."

"Why are you happy about that?"

"Because I'm pretty sure he's planning some elaborate engagement thing."

Kayla stopped in her tracks. "What?" she screeched.

Dinah giggled. "Yup. He thinks he's so subtle too. It's adorable. I mean, it's also driving me crazy because I have no idea when he's actually going to do it so I'm always halfway on edge, but it's mostly adorable."

"Dinah." Kayla didn't know why she felt so teary. It was just . . . God, they were getting old. Jobs and heartaches and *marriage*. "You're getting married."

Dinah, cool as a cucumber Dinah, looked a little teary herself. "Well, if he ever actually asks me anyway." She sniffled a little. "And I know I'm totally jumping the gun, but you'll be my maid of honor, right?"

Then they both started crying in earnest, and it was such a better cry than last night or this morning. This wasn't about being sad or vaguely dissatisfied. This was all about being so happy for someone she loved.

She pulled away from Dinah, realized they were standing in the middle of the stairwell hugging and crying. "Come on. We can cry inside."

"And drink, right?" Dinah asked in a squeaky voice.

"Damn straight."

Kayla walked with Dinah up the stairs, but nearly ran into her when Dinah stopped short at the top of the stairwell.

"Oh," Dinah said, an odd tone to her voice.

Kayla sniffled looking over at the door where Dinah had stopped midstep. "Oh," Kayla repeated herself.

Liam got to his feet, shoving his hands in his pockets. "Um, hi. I need to talk to you."

Part of her wanted that too. A very big part. But he couldn't just stomp on her heart one night and then show up the next expecting to get whatever he wanted.

"We're busy."

"This is important."

Kayla lifted her chin, pointing between her and Dinah. "So is this."

Dinah reached out and squeezed her hand. "Why don't I go home?"

"But—"

Dinah shook her head. "Get your shit straightened out, Kay. We'll celebrate after it actually happens, okay? I want your head in the game for it." Then she pulled Kayla into a hug and squeezed. "Just work it out, or cut it off for good," she whispered. "Don't let it keep dragging out, okay?"

Kayla sniffled again and nodded as Dinah released her. After one last arm squeeze, Dinah disappeared down the stairs and Kayla stood in the breezeway with Liam.

Her heart *hurt*. A sharp, painful ache in her chest. She hadn't had time to build up any kind of defense against him. Everything with them had all happened so fast, and she needed time to sort it out.

She could live without him—she knew that—but she needed a little bit more time to feel like that was the best alternative. Right now living without him just sucked.

"I don't want to do this right now." She grabbed her keys and moved for her door.

But he stepped in front of her. "I do," he said firmly.

She knew she should meet his steady gaze with the most condescending, imperious look she could manage. She should tell him to go to hell. Instead, she stared blindly at his chest. Her throat was tight and she felt like crying *again*, and it was so damn infuriating that she would cry again.

Again and again and again, over this. "Butt face."

"I'm sorry did you just . . . say . . . Did you just call me a butt face?"

She covered her face with her hands and let out an irritated groan. "I don't want to do this! I want you to leave." She blew out a breath, forcing herself to look at him. He looked tired. Beat down. "How's your Dad?" she asked, because she might think he was a butt face, but she didn't want him to be a sad one.

"Everything looks good."

"I'm glad. Really."

"I know."

"Now can you please go?" she asked, perilously close to tears.

"No."

She wanted to stomp her feet and push him. Instead, she went for a low blow. "I really think it'd be best for poor Aiden if you did, don't you?"

He ran his tongue over his top teeth and let out a breath. "I get that I deserved that." He kept that unreadable blue gaze on her. "But I'm not going anywhere until we talk."

"Why are you making this hard on me?" she demanded, trying to blink back the tears. "Last night wasn't bad enough, now you're trying to make it worse?"

"I know you're mad at me, and I know I fucked up, but I don't think we automatically stopped loving each other because we had a fight."

"Sure, but maybe I don't want to love you," she threw at him, crossing her arms over her chest.

His hand dropped and he inhaled sharply, standing so unnaturally still for a few seconds she was almost afraid to breathe.

He wiped his hand over his mouth and beard, his throat working hard to swallow. She had to stare at his throat, because on his face was a kind of pain that even mad at him she regretted having put there.

She wanted to run away. She wanted to hide. She wanted to sweep all this *feeling*—hurt and fear and fury—into some dark corner. She wanted it so bad she could hardly see straight, but there was this little piece of her reminding her of what he'd said last night.

About her running away, and he hadn't been right, exactly. She hadn't run away last night by ending things, but right now she was running away from what Dinah had suggested—figure it out or cut it off. She wanted to hide from it, wait for it to go away, and that just wasn't an option.

"Let me tell you about this morning, and then if you still feel that way, I'll go," he said, his voice little more than a rough scrape, his throat still moving as if he found it as hard to breathe evenly as she did.

Though everything in her screamed to refuse, she forced herself to nod. Figure it out or cut it off. This had to be handled, not run away from, even if the hardest part was the fact that he'd been the best example of standing up and taking care of things she'd ever seen.

Grandmother and Dinah bulldozed through, and Dad swept things out of the way or manipulated his way to get what he wanted, but Liam stepped in and solved problems and really helped people. He cared beyond himself.

That was half of why she was standing here crying as she unlocked her door and pushed it open though. Because she admired his ability to *fix*, she just hated his inability to draw any boundaries with it.

She wiped her face with her palms as she stepped into her apartment. She heard him follow and close the door but she didn't turn around to face him. She hugged herself and tried to figure out what it was she wanted from this.

From him.

To end it. She had to end it. This was Liam's pattern, and it wasn't going to change. Working things out would only bring them right back here, and it was too much hurt. It was way too hard. She had to end things now with complete and utter certainty.

"I was wrong last night," Liam said, his voice low and sure. Never in her entire life had Kayla heard someone admit being wrong with such a sincere certainty.

She glanced over her shoulder at him, and he stood there, eyes steady on hers, so . . . sturdy and certain. She looked away again.

"You were right, and the funny thing is, you're not the first person to accuse me of my helping priorities being a little skewed."

"So why should I think what I said actually mattered if no one's ever gotten through to you?"

"Because you were the first person who really truly mattered to accuse me of it."

Her arms began to shake even as she held herself tighter. She wanted to be strong enough to say it wasn't enough. She wanted to be strong enough to know that ending it was the only possibility for them to both be happy.

But those words undid all of her certainty.

Kayla didn't say anything. She kept standing there in the middle of her living room with her back to him. Holding herself, something like a tremor going through her body, but she made no other reaction to his words.

He didn't know if he was getting anywhere, and that clawed at him, but his only choice here was to keep powering forward.

Maybe he couldn't fix *everything*, but he still had to believe there were some things he could—and should—fix.

"It turns out when someone you love says something you don't want to hear, it's a lot harder to dismiss, and then my grandmother sort of reinforced what you said, and it's really, really hard to deny the truth when two people are forcing you to look at it at the same time."

She turned to face him, but nothing about the expression on her face was reassuring. Her eyebrows were drawn together, and her lips were pressed into a firm, disapproving line.

"I'm glad . . ." She cleared her throat and it killed him to see and hear that kind of pain in her. Pain he'd put there. "I think it's great you think we're right, because I happen to agree, but I don't see how it changes anything."

"How can it not change anything?" he demanded, trying to tamp down the frustration that was starting to weave in with all the hurt and fear. He knew he'd made a mistake, but only for a couple hours. She couldn't honestly be ready to end this because he'd . . .

"Talk is cheap," she said firmly, looking him in the eye. And tears swam there or he might have been felled completely by those words. "It's easy to say that I'm right. But knowing I'm right doesn't mean you won't jump to help Aiden at the expense of yourself the next time your mom asks."

"I told her," Liam gritted out, holding on to his temper. "I told Mom I wouldn't do this anymore. That I wasn't going to break up with you, not even for pretend. I told her that she needed to let Aiden try and fix himself."

"And she took that well?"

"Of course not."

Kayla inhaled carefully, shaking her head and looking away from him. "I don't want to be the thing that screws up your family. I don't . . . It isn't even all about Aiden. I mean, that's a lot of it, but it's not the only place you . . . I'd never want to be the thing you sacrifice yourself over, and I don't think I can trust you on that."

"I'm trying to realize there can be a balance, Kayla." He wanted to move close, to touch her, to get *through* to her, but she held herself like she was fragile, and he hated that he'd put that there. "I like helping people. I like fixing things. I can't change that about myself, but I think I can change how often I do those things without thinking about the consequences. I never wanted to lose you. If I'd thought for even a minute about how you'd feel about pretending to break things off, I never would have asked you to do it. I was blinded by . . ."

"Your need to fix things." She pressed her fingers to her temples. "I think you're misunderstanding me, because I get it. I get you. I know you want to help, and I know it comes from a good place, but that doesn't necessarily make you a very good bet in the whole significant-other department." She swallowed, a few tears spilling over. "I love you, Liam. I do. But I can't be the partner who says, yeah, it's fine, go help everyone else."

"Maybe I was looking for the partner who would tell me to stop," he returned, each word feeling like a shard of glass was scraping against his throat.

She let out a little sob at that, the tears falling more freely even as she tried to wipe them away, and he couldn't let that stand—not for boundaries or because she wanted him to. He crossed to her and pulled her into his arms.

She cried into his chest, and though she didn't move her arms around him, she didn't use them to push him away either. She leaned against him, and she cried, and he knew he had to keep moving forward, keep working—not to fix this but to make this.

"Remember when you told me your family treated you like decoration? I would never, Kayla. I couldn't. I *need* you, and I think you need me." He pulled her back so he could look her in the eye. "I know I'm not perfect. Sometimes you might have to remind me to step back, but what I'm saying is I'd listen. I'll always listen, and we may disagree, but I will always listen to you. I don't want to be apart.

I don't want to lose you. I *love* you, and I'm not perfect but damn if I'll make the same mistake twice once I realize it. I'll fix whatever I break."

"I don't need you to fix anything. Not my sink or me or you. Not us," she said on a whisper, but it wasn't a refusal, and she didn't step away.

"Okay, so maybe we agree to *make* something. Together. And when you make something with someone sometimes you don't agree on the direction, or maybe you have to go back and sand down some jagged edges, but you talk, and you decide together what the next step is."

She didn't say anything so he reached into his back pocket and pulled out the gift he'd brought, wrapped up in a paint-splattered cloth from his workshop. "I've been, uh, working on this the past few days, the very few moments we haven't been together, and I went home this afternoon and finished it before I came over." He held it out to her.

"What is it?" she asked skeptically.

He took her hand and placed the lump of cloth and wood into it. "Look."

She swallowed, her eyes red and tears still rolling down her cheeks and off her chin. She unraveled the cloth until the item came into view.

Her eyes went a little wide as she held it out of the cloth. "It's a lovespoon," she whispered.

"So, I, um, took a few liberties with the symbols and—"

"There's a bear."

"Two bears. The smiling one and the, er, frowning one."

She stared at the lovespoon with wide, unblinking eyes. "Like my figurines."

"Well, yeah."

She traced her hands over the outline of the spoon. He'd poured a lot of himself into the shape, into the carvings, into the meaning of it, and it meant more than he'd ever be able to articulate that she seemed to appreciate it.

"No one's ever . . ." She shook her head, her voice cracking on the *ever*.

"Paid such close attention?"

She blinked up at him as if amazed by the fact he could finish that sentence, but of course he could. "I know, because it's the same for me. No one, Kayla. I think I've been waiting for you, and I will never take that for granted."

"I was really determined to break up with you, Liam," she said, her voice squeaky and strained. Her mouth worked, her breath going in and out in little shaky bursts. "But how do you break up with the guy who gives you a lovespoon?"

"I don't know, but I'll make you a million more if it ups my chances of keeping you."

She let out a little watery laugh. "I . . . I just want what's best for both of us."

"I do, too. I think we're better together. Don't you?"

This time she stepped toward him, sliding her arm around his neck and pulling him against her. "I do," she whispered, holding him close and tight. "I really do."

He wrapped his arms around her, held her tight, even with the spoon between them. "I never wanted to lose you, Kay."

"I know," she said, her words muffled in his shoulder. "And I hope you know I never needed to be more important than Aiden or your family. I just wanted to be *as* important."

"You are. You absolutely are. And if you ever feel like you aren't, you—"

"Say it. Not run away from it." She tipped her head back and smiled at him. "Yeah, we are definitely better together."

There was nothing truer in his life than the fact that Kayla Gallagher made it better, and he would do whatever it took to make sure that lasted a lifetime.

Epilogue

"How do we have so much stuff?" Kayla complained, making a circle in her brand-new living room surrounded by boxes. "I'm pretty sure half this shit is Liam's tools."

"Damn it, Aiden, I told you not to swear in front of Zane," Aiden's girlfriend, Zoe, said, clapping her hands over her ten-year-old's ears.

"You just said damn it," Aiden replied, throwing his hands in the air.

Aiden had started dating Zoe a few months ago. No one was more surprised than Kayla that Zoe and her son had seemed to be the kind of calming influence Aiden had been in desperate need of.

And, even stranger, Mrs. Patrick had warmed up to Kayla considerably in those few months as well. She still tended to overstep and ask Liam for things that weren't necessarily fair, but any time Liam was uncertain, he came to her and they talked.

Kayla had always trusted Liam, but she could admit now in retrospect she'd been careful in those first few months after they'd gotten back together. She'd been waiting for the other shoe to drop, for Liam to overextend himself again.

He hadn't. There'd been those few unfair requests from his mother, but he always came right to her. And it wasn't like he was asking for her permission or approval, or like she was checking up on everything they did. It was a conversation. It was a *partnership.*

She'd come to the realization one night she'd been hanging out with Dinah helping with wedding plans that she was just . . . happy, and it was silly to undermine that with doubts.

And since then, everything had been a little easier, even the disagreements. Even spending time with his family. She wasn't afraid anymore, and that made things with Aiden and Mrs. Patrick easier too.

"All right, my big strong men, now that we've unloaded everything, who wants to go get some dinner?" Mrs. Patrick asked, linking arms with Aiden and Zane.

"You guys go ahead. We'll see you Sunday at Grandma's," Liam said.

Both Liam's parents looked at him kind of funny, and Kayla couldn't help but look at him a little funny herself. They'd been moving stuff from her place and his all day, and she was starving.

But Aiden and his crew, and Liam's parents, filed out, leaving Kayla and Liam alone in *their* house.

Okay, maybe it wasn't so bad. They'd picked out a house closer to her job, and with a huge backyard that would eventually allow them to build Liam a workshop. It was a little rundown, but both she and Liam had already put in a lot of work.

"You and Dinah did a great job with all the painting," Liam said, winding his way around the array of boxes, closer to her.

Kayla looked around. "We did, didn't we." She grinned at him. "You better have some food around here."

"I do," he replied. "I just wanted to get something out of the way first."

She rolled her eyes. "I'm all for christening the house with sex, but I am *starving*."

He chuckled, pulling something out of his pocket. "I didn't mean sex. Yet."

"Then what did you . . ." She stopped abruptly as he pulled the little velvet box out of his pocket and placed it in the center of one of the boxes between them. "Oh." She swallowed at the sudden lump in her throat. "That's a ring box."

"Yes."

"You're proposing."

"Well, you know my grandmother is losing her shit over us living in sin, so I thought I'd make it official."

"For your grandmother?" she replied, trying to scowl at him even though she knew he was joking.

"Yes. No other reason at all," he replied deadpan, but then he softened. "I would have done it that night you took me back this spring, but I wanted a real ring. The perfect ring, and I needed to save up a little for that."

"You didn't go overboard, did you?"

"No, I said perfect, not overboard. Now, are you going to open it or what?"

She frowned but took the box with shaking hands. It wasn't exactly a surprise, but it was still a *moment*. A big one. She opened the box and then glared at Liam as she pulled the contents out. "This is my smiling bear, not a ring."

He grinned. "Oh, is it?" He patted down his pockets. "Whoops. A little mix-up." He pulled a silver band from his pocket, the small but—he was right—perfect diamond winking at the top. He moved through the maze of boxes until he was in front of her, and then he got down on one knee.

She'd done a very admirable job of not crying yet, but that about did it. Him on his knee, holding the ring out to her, looking up at her with all the love in the world on his face.

"Kayla Gallagher, I love you. I want to build a life with you—a marriage, a family. Will you marry me?" he asked, and all joking and feigned casualness were gone from his expression, from his voice. His throat worked and he held out that beautiful ring, this wonderful man who'd been waiting for her.

Just as she'd been waiting for him. "Yes," she managed to squeak out. "I want all of those things with you."

He slid the ring onto her finger and then was up on his feet, taking her mouth with his. The kiss was hard and a little desperate, as if he'd been nervous. She smoothed her hands over his beard, accepting that harshness with all the softness and love she had.

"You sure we need to eat before we do the christening?" he murmured against her mouth.

"Well . . . maybe eating can wait." Before she even got the full sentence out of her mouth, he'd lifted her up and was carrying her through the maze of boxes to their bedroom—theirs—and to their future.

And now . . .
Read on for a preview of
MESS WITH ME
by
Nicole Helm
Available in September 2017 wherever books and ebooks are sold.

And in case you missed Dinah's story,
a second preview follows of
SO WRONG IT MUST BE RIGHT
by Nicole Helm
Available from Lyrical

Chapter One

Sam Goodall knew an ambush was coming. He'd known it for approximately three days and had made himself exceedingly scarce. He appeared at the cabin that headquartered Mile High Adventures with just enough time to get ready before he guided his next excursion, and no time to have conversations with anyone.

He was a quick man, an agile man, and he'd spent the past five years putting nearly all his effort into being a silent partner in Mile High Adventures, taking on the riskiest and most challenging trips, and mostly staying out of the way. He could disappear easily and quickly and hoped his streak would continue until whatever was being planned for him fizzled out.

Five years ago his best friends, Brandon and Will Evans, had lured him from a fishing boat in Alaska back to his home state and their once-shared dream of this outdoor adventure company, but they hadn't lured him back to the land of normal.

That land had been demolished a long time ago.

"Sam!"

Sam winced at the feminine lilt of Lilly Preston's voice. He liked Lilly well enough, despite her ever-present Grunt Jar and chatter and questions, but this would be none of those things.

This was only the beginning of the ambush.

"On my way out," he grumbled, barely pausing in his quick retreat out the back. His Jeep was parked in the front, and all he needed to do was turn the corner and disappear and he'd be safe for another day.

"I'm really not feeling up to chasing after you, Sam."

He cursed under his breath. Though he had no qualms about running from a pregnant woman, he knew Lilly would have no qualms about following him, and if she did something stupid like trip and fall, Brandon would likely kill Sam where he stood.

Which actually might be better than whatever was waiting for him.

Still, he stopped. He slowly turned to face the bright pop of color that was Lilly, Mile High's public relations specialist. She was excellent at her job, a good fit for Brandon, and, most of all, she usually let Sam keep to himself. He liked her.

He glowered down at her, arms crossed over his chest regardless of any like.

Lilly merely smiled serenely. "Have dinner with us."

"No."

She pursed her lips before responding through gritted teeth. "It wasn't an invitation."

"Still no."

She grunted, and his scowl loosened. "I believe that means you owe a dollar to the Grunt Jar."

Her hands curled into fists, her quicksilver-blue eyes flashing with temper. "Sam Goodall, you are the most frustrating part of this business, and this business includes *Skeet*, of all people."

"Thank you," he replied earnestly.

"You don't even know who I wanted you to come to dinner with, or why."

"Brandon and Will, so you three can ambush me with whatever you've been whispering and plotting all week."

Her mouth dropped open and she blinked. "For someone who's never here, you're remarkably astute."

"Goodbye, Lilly. I'll see you tomorrow." Or he'd avoid her tomorrow. Time would tell.

"Sam." She exhaled loudly as he began to walk away. "We need your help."

He didn't stop, didn't pause, didn't even hesitate. "No, you don't," he returned, and kept on walking.

When Sam woke up the next morning, he scowled. Something was off. He knew the typical sounds of the small clearing high on the mountain where he'd built his cabin, and something wasn't right.

The stillness of the air up here had been interrupted by something. The usual summer chatter of birds and animals had stopped. Sam blinked at the darkness outside his window. It was too early for much of anything to be an interruption.

Apparently the ambush had come to call.

He swung off the tiny mattress that was shoved into the corner of the big square room that was his home. The only other room in the cabin was a small bathroom off to the back.

He didn't live primarily off the grid for any moral reasons, any grand desire to save the environment or live some authentic simple life that would bring him closer to spiritual enlightenment. He did it because it felt necessary, and because it kept people away, and probably for a few other reasons he refused to spend any time considering.

Pulling on a T-shirt, Sam grumbled to himself. He shoved his feet into his boots, and when he stepped outside into the pearly dawn of a summer morning, he swore. Loudly.

"Good morning to you too, sunshine," Will Evans greeted cheerfully. He and Brandon stood leaning casually against Will's Jeep in the middle of Sam's yard.

Though the Evans brothers were twins, and looked remarkably alike, especially when sporting beards, the brothers were nothing short of opposites. Which Sam had always supposed kept them from killing each other.

Once upon a time, Sam had been the instigator of trouble in their little group, Will always the willing follower, Brandon frequently the voice of reason. But things had changed for Sam, and he'd only agreed to return to Colorado and start this business with his friends because Will and Brandon had accepted those changes.

"Go away," Sam grumbled, running his hands through his sleep-tangled hair. He needed a haircut, and a shave, but his unkempt appearance kept people at bay. Customers he guided tended not to ask too many questions of the hairy, grumpy yeti. A description that bothered him not at all.

"Stop being a coward, Sam. We've got a favor to ask." Brandon's reasonable tone scraped against the peaceful quiet of dawn.

"I don't do favors."

Will rolled his eyes. "Yes, we know. You're very gruff and scary. Now stop being so damn difficult and hear us out."

"Why should I waste your time and mine? I've got things to do." Which wasn't a lie. He had a schedule, living primarily off the grid meant anytime he wasn't working at Mile High he was working at the complex task of living stripped of most modern conveniences.

He had laundry to do by hand, firewood to chop for heat, and a mind to keep occupied in solitary, physical pursuits.

"You owe us. You know you do." Brandon's voice was quiet but tense and brooked no argument.

Sam gritted his teeth, hating to be reminded of just how much he owed the Evans brothers. They'd saved him, he had no doubt of that. He was just more than a little shocked they'd stoop so low as to use it against him. "Didn't expect that one to be thrown in my face."

"We didn't expect you to be such a dick about something so important, before you even know what it is," Will returned, a relaxed ease to his tone.

"You're alive because of us, Sam." Brandon was all edge and fury, a direct opposite to his brother.

"Who says I wanted to be kept alive?" he grumbled.

"Yourself," Will replied simply. "You'd be dead if you wanted to be."

Just because it was the truth didn't mean Sam particularly wanted it pointed out to him. "Fine. Talk. But I've got work to do." He stomped toward the back, any reference to a past he'd rather forget poking at every angry, ungenerous, destructive impulse he'd ever had.

He'd had a hell of a lot of those.

Brandon and Will followed him, and despite Will's calm demeanor, tension and stress radiated off both men.

"We need you to act as intermediary," Brandon said, wasting no time, as much because he wasn't a man to prevaricate as because Sam wouldn't stick around for any fluff.

"Between what and what?"

"We want to offer Hayley a position with Mile High," Will stated, obviously taking the role of explainer so Brandon's head didn't explode from trying not to demand something. "She refuses to talk with us. She's barred any attempt to speak with her. But she's still here, in Gracely. That's got to mean something."

"What the hell do I have to do with your family drama?"

"We need an intermediary," Brandon repeated, the way he was grinding his teeth audible across the yard as Sam picked up an armload of wood that he'd take inside to heat his stove. God knew he'd need coffee after this.

"Between you and your half sister? I'm the last man to ask."

"No. You're the *only* man to ask. You're our partner."

"Silent partner." Sam stalked back to the cabin's entrance. He had no time for this, no patience for this. Brandon and Will should know better than to try to manipulate him into *anything* that had to do with family let alone sisters—even if the mysterious Hayley Winthrop was only their sister by half.

"You can be as silent as you want. After you offer her a job," Brandon said as if it were a foregone conclusion.

"And train her. If she takes it."

Sam whirled on them, and he knew the sizzling anger wasn't appropriate for the situation, but they'd poked at every sore spot he had, far before he'd been ready to let it roll off his shoulders. What he owed, how he'd been saved, and worst of all *family*. "No." He wasn't sure if he yelled it or if he growled it.

Brandon cursed and stalked to Will's Jeep, and Sam should have been relieved. He should have been happy it hadn't come to blows, but he found himself itching for a fight. Mostly because of this whole thing, but at least a little partly because of the edgy feeling that had been dogging him for weeks.

There wasn't enough work to keep his mind engaged lately, which didn't make any sense because it was the same work there always was, and summer was high season. He was busy and challenged and yet something had been under his skin like a splinter for a while.

Yeah, a fight would have been nice. He wouldn't have had to think about that.

So he glared at Will, but Will only shook his head sadly.

"It's beneath you, Sam. All of this."

"Right back at you, Will." He didn't even have to give Will a meaningful look for that barb to hit. No matter how close the three of them had once been, they all had their secrets. And they all had their no-go zones.

This "favor" was Sam's "no-go zone" and Brandon and Will had both known it before they'd even set up this ambush. They shouldn't be pissed that Sam had been an ass. They had to have known this would happen.

But no matter how much Sam tried to convince himself of that, he went through the rest of the day feeling like a complete and utter tool.

* * *

The tool feeling didn't magically dissipate all through the afternoon. Sam guided a kayaking group, got irrationally irritated any time he had to repeat an instruction, and just narrowly missed exploding at an idiot who overturned his kayak.

Normally, despite his lack of charm or cheer, he was a helpful and informative—if disinterested—guide. Calmness and distance had become something of Sam's hallmark. Oh, he was gruff and grumpy on occasion, but the kind that caused people to give him nicknames and develop an elaborate, tragic backstory about him.

He was 99 percent certain the customers on this expedition just thought he was an arrogant prick. Which was bad business and simply not the man he'd turned himself into.

He had to shake this dogged *wrong* feeling, and the only way he knew how to do that was with physical activity. Since he had to get his shit straight with Brandon and Will, that could only mean one thing.

Once he returned from the kayak excursion and cleaned up, Sam collected three sets of climbing gear. It'd be nearly sunset even if they did one of the easier climbs, but he needed this edgy, destructive feeling inside of him *gone*.

So he strode into the office of Mile High Adventures. Skeet, the old man who acted as something between troll and receptionist, greeted him with a grunt and Sam returned it, but he didn't pause. He headed straight for the back, and luckily Brandon, Will, and Lilly were huddled in the main room looking over brochures or pictures or something.

It was a cozy, homey place, full of dark woods and thick rugs. Even before Lilly had stamped her presence on everything, the walls had been decorated with mountain prints and cheerful sayings about the outdoors.

The furniture in the main room was all dark brown leather couches, situated around a giant fireplace that dominated the room. It wasn't lit today in the middle of summer, and Lilly had covered the entrance with a large bouquet of wildflowers and greenery.

Brandon, Will, and Lilly looked like the picture-perfect family or group of friends, and Sam ignored the familiar pang that hadn't dogged him in a while.

He dropped the climbing equipment in front of the twins, waiting till three pairs of eyes were on him. "If you can both beat me to the top, you win."

Will and Brandon exchanged a look while Lilly stared at Sam as if he'd lost his mind. "Beat you to the top of what?" she asked.

"So we both have to beat you?" Brandon demanded, always one to get the rules lined up before they did anything.

"Both of you."

"And who's the judge if it's close?"

"If it's that close, I'll forfeit." Because while Will and Brandon were adept climbers, Sam was usually the one to lead those expeditions, which gave him more practice and more skill.

Brandon and Will began to stand, and Lilly all but spluttered. "What on earth . . . Explain this to me."

"Rock climbing. We'll just do, what, the south cliff face?" At Sam's nod, Brandon looked back toward his girlfriend. "No big deal."

"No big deal?" Lilly's eyebrows drew together in two angry points. "You're not actually going to agree to that!"

Will and Brandon shrugged in tandem, and Lilly turned her glare to Sam. "You're going to risk your neck trying to climb the rock face of a *mountain* the fastest, instead of just do this favor like a good friend?"

Sam didn't say anything to Lilly's glare or accusation. He found that silence was almost always the most effective answer when it came to the force of nature that was Lilly.

"Bran . . ."

"It's tradition," Brandon replied before Lilly could argue further. "Rock climbing races have solved many an argument. It's perfectly safe." He pressed a kiss to her temple before collecting one set of gear Sam had dropped. "We should be back by dark."

"We'll wear headlamps just in case," Will joked, which helped Lilly's outrage not at all.

"You're going *now*?" she all but screeched, hopping to her feet. "Of all the pseudo-macho, irresponsible, foolish—"

"Just think, it'll give you carte blanche on finalizing the new brochures," Brandon offered.

Lilly whirled. "It'll give me carte blanche on your corpse," she said stalking down the hallway and then slamming the door to her office.

"I'm going to pay for that."

Will made an unmistakable whip sound and just narrowly ducked out of Brandon's reach and a punch to the gut.

"I'm going to kick both your asses," Brandon said.

"Side wagers, then?" Will asked cheerfully. He and Brandon argued about a side bet while they loaded up Sam's Jeep with the climbing equipment and drove to the south cliff face where they held most of their rock climbing training. It was an easy to moderate climb, good for teaching people on.

Or, in this case, good for a speed challenge.

They got out of the Jeep, Brandon and Will trading good-natured trash talk. It hit a little hard, all this . . . Well, it was very much like those "old days" that Sam did his best to forget.

"It's been a while," Brandon murmured as they got into their gear.

Sam didn't meet Brandon's discerning gaze, and he immediately regretted doing something from *before,* but . . .

It was an easier apology, this gesture, than an actual apology. A little competition Sam wouldn't win would give the twins what they wanted, a nod to the old times would be an apology for not agreeing in the first place.

The Evans brothers got what they wanted, and Sam didn't have to say much.

"All right, ready?" At everyone's assenting nod, Will counted off, and at his "go" they each took a different path up to the top of the cliff face.

The climb was steady and challenging without being overwhelming. Sam could have pushed harder, and he had no doubt he could have beaten Brandon and Will—if not easily, definitively. But . . . he didn't push. He was careful, overly so, and when both men reached the top before he did, he didn't even feel a twinge at the loss.

The three of them rappelled down in silence, and when they reached the bottom they all sat on the ground for a few minutes to catch their breath.

"You let us win, didn't you?"

Sam watched the sky above them darken, took slow breaths as stars twinkled to life. He still didn't want to do the damn favor, sticking his nose in the tricky family business that involved the half sister the Evans brothers had recently found out about.

Sam could think of few things he wanted to do less than this. But once upon a time, he'd had nothing except rock bottom, pain, and guilt. The Evans brothers had given him the tools to climb out of rock bottom. They'd put him on that fishing boat, and then they'd brought him back to Colorado.

They couldn't fix what was really wrong with him. No one could. But they'd kept him from complete self-destruction, and while he didn't know Hayley Winthrop at all, he thought a sister probably deserved to know her brothers when they were men as good as Will and Brandon.

And maybe fixing one sibling relationship will—

He couldn't let that thought go any further so he got to his feet. "Let's head back so Lilly can relax. Then you can tell me what you need me to do."

He didn't wait for the brothers to come up with a response. He grabbed his gear and walked to the Jeep.

He wasn't fixing anything. He was acting as a facilitator. Because he owed the Evans brothers. That was it. He would do what he had to, and then they would leave him in peace again.

Because peace was all he was after.

SO WRONG IT MUST BE RIGHT

Chapter One

"You're not still emailing with that guy!"

Dinah looked up from her phone and blinked at her cousin. It took a minute to get her bearings and remember that Kayla was waiting on her to get started.

"Actually I was reading up on Trask. I found an article that might explain his reluctance to sell."

Kayla snatched her phone away, then frowned at the screen. "It is sick that you get the same look on your face reading those pervy emails as you do reading stuff for work."

"I don't know what you're talking about," Dinah replied primly. Okay, maybe she did know what Kayla meant, and maybe it was a little sick, but Gallagher's Tap Room was Dinah's blood. The Gallagher family had moved to St. Louis over a century ago and built a little pub on the very land beneath the concrete floor under her feet. It was everything to her, and if she got a little excited about that? It was fine.

Kayla gestured toward the back door and Dinah stood to follow. Meeting with Trask was going to be it. The moment she finally proved to Uncle Craig and the board she was ready to take over as director of operations.

Being Uncle Craig's "special assistant" had turned out to mean little more than being his bitch, and while she'd worked to be the best damn bitch she could be, she was ready for tradition to take over. From the very beginning, the eldest Gallagher in every generation took over. These days, the title was director of operations, but it was all the same. And she was the eldest Gallagher of the eldest Gallagher. She'd been told her whole life that this would be hers when her father retired, or, as it turned out to be with Dad, abandoned everyone and everything in the pursuit of his midlife crisis.

It was time. Dinah was ready, and getting some crazy urban farmer to sell his land next to Gallagher's for the expansion was going to be the final point in her favor. No one would be able to deny she was ready.

Director of operations was everything she'd been dreaming about since she'd been old enough to understand what the job required. Long after she'd understood what Gallagher's meant to her family, and to her.

"So you finally stopped emailing creepy Internet dude?"

Dinah walked with Kayla down the hallway to the back exit. "He's not creepy." The guy she'd somehow randomly started emailing with after she'd tipsily commented on his Tumblr page one night wasn't creepy. He was kind of amazing.

"Dinah."

"I'm sorry. No way I'm giving that guy up. It's some of the hottest sex I've ever had."

Dinah thought wistfully over how he'd ended his last email. *And when you're at the point you don't think you can come again, I'll make sure that you do.* It might be only through a computer, but it was far superior to anything any other guy had ever said to her.

"It's fictional."

"So?"

"He's probably like a sixty-year-old perv. Or a woman, if he's really as good as you say he is."

"As you pointed out, it's fictional. Who cares?"

They stepped out into the lingering warmth of late September. The urban landscape around Gallagher's was a mix of old and new, crumbling and modern. Soon, Gallagher's was going to make sure the entire block was a testament to a city that could reinvent itself.

"What does he do, send you pictures of models? Oh, baby, check out my six-pack. Then suddenly he's claiming to be David Gandy."

"We don't trade pictures of each other or any personal information that might identify us. I mean, he knows I have freckles. I know he has a birthmark on his inner thigh, but that's about it. It is pure, harmless, sexy, sexy words."

"Geez." Kayla waved her phone in front of Dinah's face, the screen displaying a myriad of apps. "Not even Snapchat?"

"Nope. It's all very old-fashioned. Like Jane Austen. Or *You've Got Mail.* Only with sex stuff."

"Go have some real sex, Dinah."

"I do that too!" Although admittedly less and less. Maybe not for six months or so. Trying to prove herself to Uncle Craig was eating her life away, and the nice thing about a sexy email was she could read it whenever she wanted and didn't have to remember its birthday or cook it dinner. It was perfect really, except the whole do-it-yourself aspect.

But do-it-yourself had been instilled in her from a young age, no matter how false the message rang in her adulthood.

The tract of land behind Gallagher's that Uncle Craig wanted to buy was a strange sight in downtown St. Louis. Between one empty lot Uncle Craig had already bought, and an aging home with a scraggly yard that Craig was also after, a land of green emerged.

Not even green grass, but huge plants, archways covered in leaves, rows and rows of produce-bearing stems. So much green stuff the crumbling brick exterior of the old house behind it all was barely visible from where they stood in front of the chain-link fence that enclosed the property.

"It's cute. Kind of funny we're trying to get him to sell it so we can pave over it and then have a farmers' market."

Dinah had waged her own personal battle over the seemingly ironic, or at the very least incongruous, business plan her uncle had put forth, but being the black sheep of the family thanks to her dad screwing just about everything up meant Dinah didn't have a say. Even Kayla, as sustainability manager, adding her opinion had done nothing to sway Craig.

So Dinah would find a way to get Mr. Hippie Urban Farmer to sell his land, and with any luck, convince him she was doing *him* a favor and sign him up for a booth for next year's market that Kayla would be in charge of. The Gallagher & Ivy Farmers' Market would be a success one way or another.

"Look, apparently from what I can tell he grew up on a real farm and his family left that one, and then he worked on some other family member's farm who sold to a developer or something. This place was his grandmother's house and over the course of the past four years he's turned it into this. So that may explain his refusing Gallagher's initial offer."

"What makes you think we can get through to him if my dad couldn't?"

"His family has a history of selling land. He should be well versed in the benefits. Surely a guy like him wants a bigger space, and the money we're offering will allow him that. Besides, we have a soul and decency on our side."

Kayla snorted. "No offense, but I'm a little glad your dad went off the deep end and I'm not the only one with a soulless Gallagher as a father."

"Gee, thanks," Dinah muttered, trying to ignore the little stab of pain. She couldn't be offended at the attack on her dad. It was warranted. They'd spent plenty of their childhood complaining about Kayla's dad being a douche. But still, it hurt. It wasn't supposed to be this way.

Oh well, what could she do? She and Kayla stepped under the archway of green tendrils and the sign that read *Front Yard Farm*. The place *was* cute. Weird, no doubt, but cute.

Before they could make it past the first hurdle of beanstalks or whatever, the door to the brick house creaked open and a man stepped onto the porch. Dinah stopped mid-step, barely registering that Kayla did too.

He was tall and lanky and wearing loose-fitting khaki-colored pants covered in dirt and a flannel shirt with sleeves rolled to the elbows over a faded T-shirt. It was the face though that really caught her attention. Sharp and angular. Fierce. Only softened by the slight curl to his dark hair, his beard obscuring his jaw line. Something about the way he moved was pure grace, and everything about his looks made Dinah's attraction hum to attention.

"He's like every hipster fantasy I've ever had come to life," Dinah whispered, clutching Kayla's arm briefly.

"Lord, yes."

The man on the stoop, with the hoe, and the flannel, and the beard—sweet Lord—stared at them suspiciously. "Can I help you two?"

Dinah exchanged a glance with her cousin, who was valiantly trying to pretend they hadn't been drooling.

"Mr. Trask?"

"Yeah."

"Hi, I'm Dinah Gallagher and this is Kayla Gallagher. We're from Gallagher's Ta—"

"Nope."

The door slammed so emphatically, Dinah jerked back. She'd barely registered the guy moving inside before he was completely gone behind that slammed door.

"Well."

"What were you saying about human decency and souls making a difference?"

Dinah started picking her way across the narrow and uneven brick path to the door. "He hasn't had a chance to see it yet. Maybe the meeting with your dad ended poorly. We'll have to mend a few fences."

"Before we buy them all," Kayla muttered. "Remember when we were kids and thought we'd be calling the shots?"

"We still will be. Just need another decade." Or two. That's how family business worked. She wasn't going to abandon it just because it was harder than she'd expected or taking longer than she'd anticipated. No, she was going to fight.

And should Kayla ever get married, Dinah would not follow in her father's footsteps and sleep with her best friend and family member's spouse.

Dinah reached the door and knocked. She didn't entertain thoughts of failing because it simply wasn't an option. Failing Gallagher's was never going to be an option.

The door remained closed. Dinah pursed her lips. This was *not* going the way she'd planned.

"Okay. Well. I won't be deterred."

"Come on, Dinah. Let's go." Kayla stood in the yard, hands shoved into the pockets of her dress. "Call him. Write him an email. I don't want him calling the cops on us. Oh, maybe you can accidentally write him one of your sex emails. That'll get his attention." She sighed, loud enough to be heard across the yard. "I would so not mind getting that guy's attention."

"I'm going to pick something." Dinah surveyed the plants surrounding her. She didn't know a lot about farmers or farming, but if he was so dead set on not selling, he obviously cared deeply about this yard of produce. So she'd lure him out that way.

"Don't! He'll call the cops."

Dinah waved her off. "I'll pick something ripe and give it back to him. I'm doing him a favor, really."

Kayla muttered something, but Dinah ignored her. She surveyed the arches of green and splashes of color—squash maybe.

Something about it all looked very familiar. Like she'd seen it . . . somewhere. Somewhere. Well, she didn't have time to dwell on that. She had to find something ripe to pick.

And since she had no idea what she was doing, that was going to be a challenge.

Carter was not falling for this dirty trick. He wasn't. If he was grinding his teeth and clenching his fists in his pockets, it was only because . . .

Aw, fuck it. She was winning. Touching his plants, his stuff, picking a damn unripe squash. He couldn't let it go even if he knew that was her plan all along.

He threw open the window, pushing his face close to the screen. "I'm calling the cops," he shouted.

"Oh, I wish you wouldn't," the brunette returned just as casual as you please. "I only want to have a civil conversation."

"Hell to the no, lady. I know what Gallagher means by civil and it's screw me six ways to Sunday and then expecting me to thank him for it."

"As you can see, *Mr.* Gallagher isn't here."

"Just because you have breasts doesn't mean I'm more inclined to talk to you." Even if they were rather distracting when she was kneeling facing his window. From his higher vantage point, he could see down the gap between fabric and skin. Dark lace against very pale skin. A few freckles across her chest and cheeks. He briefly thought of his last email from D.

Maybe we couldn't wait, and I unbutton and unzip your pants right there on your front porch.

He couldn't think about the rest of that email and maintain his irritation, so he forced it out of his mind and focused on the offending party.

Her hair was a fashionable tangle of rich reddish-brown waves. Her face was all made up with hues of pink, and the heels of her shoes sank into the mud next to his zucchini.

When she stood, wrinkling her freckled nose at him, he could see that she had long, lean legs, probably as pale and freckly as her chest, but black tights obscured them.

Which was good. This was one attraction he had no interest in pursuing. A Gallagher for fuck's sake. Of course she was gorgeous. She probably paid a lot of money to be. Her family was rolling in it.

"I'm calling the cops," he threatened again.

"Don't you think they have better things to do?"

"Listen lady—"

"All I want is ten minutes of your time, Mr. Trask. That's all. Much easier than getting the police involved."

shine
so wrong it
must be right
NICOLE HELM

credit: Callie Boyd Photography

Nicole Helm grew up with her nose in a book and a dream of becoming a writer. Nicole writes down-to-earth contemporary romance. From farmers to cowboys, Midwest to the West, she writes stories about people finding themselves and finding love in the process. When she's not writing, she spends her time dreaming about someday owning a barn. She lives with her husband and two young sons in Missouri.

Printed in the United States
by Baker & Taylor Publisher Services